The Wacky Man

Lyn G. Farrell

Legend Press Ltd, 175-185 Gray's Inn Road, London, WC1X 8UE
info@legend-paperbooks.co.uk | www.legendpress.co.uk

Print ISBN 978-1-7850795-5-9
Ebook ISBN 978-1-7850795-6-6
Set in Times. Printed in the United Kingdom by Clays Ltd.
Cover design by Simon Levy www.simonlevyassociates.co.uk

There is no doubt fiction makes a better job of the truth
Doris Lessing

Part One
Right Now

My new shrink asks me, 'What things do you remember –
about being very young?'

It's like looking into a murky river, I say. Memories flash
near the surface like fish coming up for flies. The past peeps
out, startles me, and then is gone.

I tell him it's like looking through a filthy window. I'm not
even sure if I'm looking in on the right life. If I find a gap in
the smudge I see chippy suppers, pogo sticks, flared pink jeans,
burnt fish fingers, a paper bag with three cigarettes and a single
bubble gum, 'The Irish' and the priest visiting, pet dogs and
rabbits, ferrets, my teddy, Mum's lipstick, Dad's Old Spice,
over-boiled carrots, schoolbooks covered in wallpaper, home-
brewed beer. It's like being on the *Generation Game*, I say, like
they're all going past on a conveyer belt. My shrink laughs. He
always tells me I'm very funny and not to forget how to do that.

I tell him when I sleep it's like a black hole pulling me
in. I spin blindly around inside this airless, sweaty, dark
space, tearing myself on the shards of my past and I can't see
anything. I am every age when I am in there – I am two and
five and nine and ten and twelve and we are all screaming at
something, though whether that something is the same for all
of us I don't know. I can't get us out even though I try, and I
wake up gasping.

'Tell me about your first memories,' my shrink asks me.

I don't tell him:

I hold the magic cylinder in my hands and shake it up,
down, up, down, up, down. As I shake, I dance; my tottering

7

feet make small soft dints in the pretty white powder which also covers me top to bottom as it floats down from my talc bottle to settle in the furry creases in the rug. I sing and stamp around within this beautiful white circle and I don't hear Dad enter the room. I am suddenly airborne; swinging towards the ceiling and then back down into the dust that puffs up around me as my feet hit the ground. I am turned around to face my father who is smiling and singing though I no longer remember the song. I try to grab his hand and my fingers hit the end of his cigarette. I scream and fat tears stream down into the dust and I cry out.

'Ma-ma. Ma-ma. Ma-maaaa.'

As my mother runs in I keep calling until the very moment she touches me and I sit on her lap, my throat burning, sniffling with an ashy fist crammed into my wet mouth. My father picks the talcum tube up off the hearth.

I don't tell him:

I cling, with Tommo, to my mother, my face hidden in her skirt while Dad swings his walking stick through the air like a musketeer. He lands it on Jamie's back and it makes a noise like a stick of celery snapping. I am bunched up with Tommo and Mum, against the wall in the corner of the front room.

'Please, Seamus, for the love of God...' Mum says.

I hear Jamie hit the floor and the stick still swishing. Then Dad throws the stick down and sits in his chair. There is wrestling on the TV.

'Shut fucking up,' Dad says, and we stop our snivelling chorus, all of us perfectly in time. Mum makes a fanning motion at the door as she picks Jamie up. Tommo drags me past Dad, who I bump into and he swings his hand out and slaps me once across the side of my head and I yell even though it doesn't hurt that much. Mum pushes from the rear and we exit quickly without noise. We are like an old silent movie as we leave the room, jerking along in a tangle of hands and legs.

I don't tell him:

8

I am stood in front of Dad. Mum stands by his chair as he shouts at me, spit flecks flying from his mouth. It is the day after my sixth or seventh birthday and I am wearing the pastel blue-and-pink shell necklace my aunty bought me. The pointed edges of it poke into the skin around my neck.

'Come closer, so I can get a good kick at your shins,' Dad says.

I have no words for this. I sit looking at my shrink, my school skirt itchy on my skin. It's usually late at night when memories swim up through that murky river and when they come, I lie imprisoned in my bed, afraid of my own dreams, crying like some kind of animal into the blackness.

Are you still there? Well. We know how this is going to end, don't we? I know it, and you know it, and all of *them* – Mum (though out of sight, out of mind applies there), the neighbours, the professionals. I'm just waiting for the shrink to turn up tomorrow with whatever entourage he might bring, and then they'll drag me off to some fucking kids' home with a load of other basket cases. They're coming to take me away, ha ha hee hee, as the fucking song goes. So we all know exactly where I'm headed and it's not up. I mean, I'm pulling my hair out, strand by strand, pop, pop, pop. That can't be a good sign. I hold a few hairs taut in my left hand, perpendicular to my head. I have to grasp them mid-length as my hair is so long. I isolate a single hair by using the finger and thumb on my other hand to rub away the excess ones until I am left with just one, which I stretch and pluck. If I pluck two instead of the one, the feeling is diluted across the scalp; but when I get it right I get this small, intense, perfect sensation. The hair leaves its follicle with a clear pop that prickles my ears, sends goose bumps Mexican waving up and down my arms and launches me, hovering somewhere above myself. When I pull my hair, I am no longer me but a tiny wave of electricity that zizzes, unheard, free. I'm bald down the middle of my head with long flaps of hair on either side. I've got an inverse Mohican. I can't see it – I never look at myself – I can feel it though. I like to run my fingers up and down the bald strip in the middle. It feels soft next to the grainy texture of my hair, as if that little strip of head is covered in velvet.

Look at me, sat here with the curtains permanently closed, keeping out the lights and the nosy neighbours. I live inside this room. It's never day or night or morning or afternoon. It's just something o'clock. I can feel the eyes watching me – all bloody peeking up, trying to cop a look. So I sit on the floor, in the dust. I can't remember the last time this carpet was hoovered. I prefer it down here, wedged in the shadowy narrow space between the bunk beds and the chest of drawers. I am sitting with my back against the radiator, which is cold because the heating doesn't work in this room. It's as plain as day that my little life is about to plummet so far down in the gloomy depths of the psyche, there is no way back up without a miracle – and who could believe in any of that miracle bollocks after a decade of Catholic schooling? So, I'll keep talking shit and if you've got nothing better to do, sit yourself down with your cup of tea and your morning biscuits and read on. Oh, I know that you're looking at me thinking, Thank Christ that's not me, but that's alright, I don't mind. I'm beyond caring.

What's my name? I have tons of names but my real one is Amanda May. I sound like one of the fucking Nolan sisters. My shrink just says Amanda because I asked him to. For fuck's sake, I need more fags. I'm down to my last three. Even if I smoke half at a time they'll be long gone by morning. Mum says she hates me smoking but she always buys them for me. My shrink told her not to give me fags while I'm hiding in here so she tried that once. I cried for three days and headbutted the wall. My head gave this massive crack like a whip and Mum was in the toilet and she heard it. When she came up with my dinner, she knocked and then said there was a packet of Benson's for me. She called me love. My favourite smokes are when I wake up in the morning or when I wake up in the middle of the night. If I get enough smoke into my lungs fast enough my head feels like it's swelling to the size of a hot-air balloon. I go floating off across the ceiling and I feel like I could fly away. And then I drift, quiet and slow, like a kite someone's let go. The shrink told Mum not to let Bonnie up either. He said that if I wanted to see her I had to get back into a more normal routine. I miss her tons. I used to say her name right into her ears and she'd put her head on my knee. I keep telling myself I'll sneak down for her when Mum's asleep, but I'm scared to get through all that whispering dark on my own.

My friends called me Manda. Every time a teacher said Amanda May, snarling it out from between bared teeth, I shrivelled into the centre of my clothes. Except for Mr Kramm, he always called me Terry. He said it was short for terrier because I'm small but fierce. He was a bellower but his voice went soft when he spoke to me. Not in a pervy way, like our old headmaster, just soft. He'd say, 'What masterpiece have you got for me today, Terry?' and he wasn't even taking the piss. He told me once, 'I bloody love reading your stories,' and swore just like that. It was him that brought me all these books.

Kids called me all sorts at school – all the usual unoriginal stuff you'd expect from people as thick as pigshit: fatty, fatso, Duff the scruff, scruffy Duffy, pygmy, midget. Roberts and his mates always sang 'OH-MANDY, you came for a shag COS-YOU'RE-RANDY' when I went past. Dickheads. Since the fights, some have started calling me Psycho. Not to my face anymore though – they don't dare. Joey from the gypo house up the road called me Miss Piggy, but only when he was far enough away not to get a punch. Irish gran called me Two-Ton-Tessie. My Irish uncles called me Good Gersha. My aunty Pammy called me Princess. Dad called me lots of things, but mostly he said Little English Bastard. Our Jamie and Tommo called me Poltergeist when they lived at home because I used to throw things when I got angry. I threw a glass at Jamie once; a tiny one with a picture of a four-leaf clover on it. It caught him on the side of his head and blood started spurting everywhere. They always made ghost noises at me after that, when Dad wasn't there to tell us all to shut the fuck up. They used to run after me chanting 'woooh hoooooo', and saying that things flew around the room whenever I went into it. I used to point at the scar on Jamie's temple and ask him, 'Wasn't it lucky?' It was funny back then. I had names for people too. After we went to Ireland on holiday I called Irish gran the Wicked Witch of the West because she's evil, and Keash, where she lives, is west of here. I used to call Dad Pontius Paddy because he set himself up as the judge of fucking everyone and he's a Paddy. When he used to go on about how English Catholics are heathens – just so he could stay home drinking while Mum dragged us all off to church – I started calling him Pope Seamus. One day he hammered me with his walking stick for wacking it. What's wacking it? You know, skiving, bunking off school. I starting calling him the Wacky Man because that's what we call the truant officer and Dad was whacking me for wacking it. I changed it later to Zorro because that was way funnier. And I called him Bogtrotter once, right to his face. I thought he'd break my ribs but I was just laughing there on the floor, under his boots.

Jamie's proper name is James. He's named after Dad and Grandad because James is English for Seamus. Tommo – Thomas – is called after Mum's grandad who died before Tommo was born. I'm named after Aunty Pammy, her middle name is Amanda. I wish I was called Pammy or Pamela though. Specky Kev in the shop always chanted 'Man-DAH – Man-DAH, yer-belly's-like-a-bay-windah', while I stood there waiting for whatever overpriced and out-of-date comestibles – yes, I know *words*, I'm mental, not retarded – I'd been sent for, listening to everyone in the queue snickering at me. He's a fat fucker anyway but nobody sings songs about him. 'Sticks and stones may break my bones but names will never hurt me'... Bullshit. Sticks and stones hurt from the outside in. Names hurt from the inside out. They're like really bad hiccups: they stab you in the guts and make your face go bright red. And it was exactly the same every single time I poked my pig-face out through the door – names and names and names and names.

The very last time I was in school, Mr Kramm told us all, 'Write an essay called "Me and The Future".' I wrote this:

Things like me, deformed, forgotten things, we don't have a future. We just have a day when we no longer wake up.

When I went outside, I only saw the bottom of things because my head was always bent towards the ground. I kept my hair over as much of my face as possible. The shrink says it was because I have 'extreme anxiety' but really it was so nobody could see my pig-face with my lardy cheeks and my bloody onion bulb nose. Sometimes the wind blew my hair back and I felt like someone had kicked me right in the heart. So I kept my eyes at the floor, that way I couldn't see if anyone was looking at me. I probably turned them to stone if they did, like Medusa. I walked everywhere really fast, almost running. I saw feet and legs and scuffed shoes, coat hems, the bottoms of shopping bags, insects scuttling out of cracks in the pavement, dog ends in the gutters and dog muck on the grass and blobs of old chewing gum like dirty pink coins scattered over the paths. I heard the birds, and the neighbours, other kids playing somewhere in the field. And I felt the sky. I hated it outside, it made me go funny. I had to bite the inside of my mouth in case I cried and my skin tingled like little insects were crawling up my legs and arms and I'd get all hot and sweaty and it went away, just like that, when I got back inside. You what? How long have I been in here? Do you mean in my room or in the house? I've not been outside my bedroom for ages. It must be well over a year by now because I was in the third year when I started wacking it this time around – *truanting* – from school. I used to run round the back of the sports hall and then over the fence by the mill and across the road and up Harold Avenue. Sometimes the Wacky Man – the *Truant Officer* – would appear before I got to the end and I'd not be able to run up the white path and into my home; I'd have to swerve down the snicket and along past the Spar shop to the fields and I'd have to run right through them and round God's Hill, over the stile by Ash Labs and down through the garages, which meant I'd have to leg it past Gran's house and hope Grandad didn't see me. Dad always said he had eyes like a shithouse rat. I'd be in the fifth year by now, if I wasn't in here. I had my fifteen birthday in here. That was back in April. Mum put cards next to my dinner and said through the door that one was from Tommo. There was a box of chocolates and a few new books. I ate the chocolates instead of the dinner. I took the books and left the cards. My shrink says that I've 'detached myself from the world outside'. Too bloody right I have. I know exactly what that shitty world outside is like.

Mum's just been up to give me my dinner. She leaves it on the floor just outside. She has two dogs now: Bonnie downstairs and me upstairs. She'll probably start feeding me in one of Bonnie's bowls too. You can laugh if you want, that's a joke.

At first she always tried to get me to come out. She'd say she had chocolate cake and I should pop downstairs. That it was all set out, ready, in front of the telly for me. Whenever I got to the bedroom door, I'd get that same tingling feeling like being outside. And when I got to the stairs it felt like trying to climb a steep path, even though I was trying to go down. I was out of breath without moving. It was like the time Dad took us on holiday after we'd come back home to him. I went on a Haunted House at the fairground where the steps were wobbling and rolling around and I got really dizzy. Going downstairs felt just like that and I'd stand on the top step until sweat ran down my neck and into my eyes. I'd shout, 'I'll come down later,' and she used to say, 'Please try for me love.' And then she got Jenny and Paula to call round for me all the time and they'd call up the stairs, 'Are you coming down the disco?' but I'd always say I was too tired. Mum tried to look at me last week, said she wanted to see how I was doing. When I reached out through the door for the plate, she was still stood there, gawping at me, her eyes all big, like I'm the Elephant Man. I completely lost it. I threw the plate through the door and started screaming, hammering my head with my fists over and over until she started crying. I heard her scraping the food off the wall and I said sorry through the door and it made her cry again.

Crispy pancakes and chips and peas tonight – again. Mum didn't try to talk to me tonight, just knocked, twice, like we agreed, to show that she's going downstairs. She's probably too annoyed to bother. She's had to stay in all day today for the shrink coming. When he came this afternoon, I opened the door and listened. I do that sometimes when people are talking about me. I heard her asking him if he wanted a cup of tea and him saying something about an assessment. I kept worrying that he'd know I was earwigging, that he'd smell my bad smell wafting downstairs. Then someone knocked at the front door and startled the shit out of me. I closed the door and got in bed.

What do I do in here? What the fuck do you think I do? I'm sick of answering stupid questions all the time. You keep looking at me like I'm a fucking monkey in a zoo. If I were you, I'd get out before you make me kick off. I'm going to sleep.

Hello again! What time is it? About ten-ish I reckon. Aunty Pammy bought me a watch but I smashed it up. I think I've only had about an hour's kip. Shut up a sec. Has she gone to bed? I need the bog. I can't hear anything. Jesus, I've got a headache coming. You didn't really think I'd hurt someone, did you? Don't listen to them bloody teachers. That was self-defence. It's just physics you need to look out for. I throw things when I get upset: shoes, books, plates sometimes. I only hurt myself like *that*. If I forget not to think about what I am, I get mad and punch myself around the head and face. I used to cut myself with a razor that Dad left behind but Mum begged me to give it to her. Now I just hit myself or rip out my hair or head-butt something. Why? Because I feel like I'm going to burst sometimes. God, did you hear my bones cracking, just then? I'm like a battery hen. My legs creak when I try to get my horrid fat body up. It's because I don't get enough exercise. Sometimes they go numb and I can't feel them, and when I try to get up they're all wobbly.

You asked what do I do in here. Fuck all. I used to read a lot, all through the night to keep vigil against things that might lurk when the day deserts; the bare light bulb my wand to ward off evil. If I open a book now, the words jig about all over the page and I can't follow them. My eyes water all the time anyway. Mum says it's all the muck and tells me please sit on the bed not the floor; but the bed's too high and I feel like people are trying to look at me through the curtains, so I only get on the bed when I need to sleep. I go from bed to corner to toilet to corner to bed. The stairs are the furthest I've got in a long time. That was going abroad for me. And when I'm not 'travelling', I pull out my hair, like I've said. Not tearing it out in chunks, the way I do when I've gone off on one – just pulling it, a single hair at a time. So that is what I do. I eat, shit and sleep. Or I sit through the night and I pull out my hair, pop, pop, pop.

Part Two
Way Back Then

．ᴥ

Joe McGinnis, who has put them up in fine style since they landed in Dublin yesterday, drives them to Seamus' parents' cottage to join the convoy of dark suits and bright dresses assembling for his sister's wedding. Before Seamus has got the gate open, people come rushing over to him in a chorus of 'hullos'. Everyone is talking to him at once until a balding man says, 'Jeysus, let the dog see the rabbit would yous.' When they step back, the man yells, 'Ah, Seamus, Seamus!' and slaps him again and again across the back.

'Barbara,' Seamus says, 'this is me eldest brother, Sean. Sean, this is me fiancée, Barbara.'

'Hullo there, Bar-bara,' Sean says. Seamus rattles off the names of his brothers and sisters at Barbara, pointing to one after the other of the men and women circling them and talking ten to the dozen. As he says their name, they dip forward and stick out their hands. She juggles names as long as she can but as the roll call goes on and on, she feels them dropping at her feet. A frail-looking man appears in a gap made by the group shuffling sideways and Seamus puts a hand on his shoulder and draws him out.

'Barbara, this is me dad.'

'Call me Tommy now, do you hear?' the man says, and puts out a thin, shaky hand to her, 'Welcome to you and welcome home, son.'

'Mammy, mammy – here's Seamus with his fiancée,' one of the sisters, who might be called Marie, shouts over all the commotion.

The mother walks down the path and stands in front of them. Seamus only has time to say hello before he and his father are dragged away by his brothers over to the yellow patch of grass where the rest of the men have reassembled, smoking and joking. His mother looks at Barbara as if she is watching flies thronging around a cow's backside. She is an angry-looking woman, red-faced and stout as an ox. Two of Seamus' other sisters, one is Orlaigh, Barbara thinks, though god knows who the other one is, stand beside their mother as she regards Barbara. They are also hefty, with the same thick jaw that has a sneer hanging off it. The three of them form an odd tableau in front of the lopsided, blue-painted house.

'How-ya?' his mother says. The greeting is shot at Barbara like a bullet. Barbara put her hand out and the mother looks down at the outstretched limb as if it were a snake. She looks Barbara straight in the eye and turns on her heels. The daughters, one on either arm, smirk and spin right around with their mother.

Before she has had chance to react she is surrounded by three young women who have come tearing out of the house. One of them is Might-be-Marie, who says, 'Here she is – his fiancée.' She says the word proudly and the girls crowd round. All of them, like her, are teenagers, though at the younger end to her. They stare at her as if she were a movie star dropped in. She is hugged by each in turn, who fire off their names and then bombard her with questions about 'Would her dress be from London or would it be Manchester?' and 'What brand is her lipstick?' The few answers she tries sink without trace under their unrelenting commentary as they feel her gloved hands and pass round her handbag for inspection. One pats her glossy black hair, scooped up in a mini-beehive, and asks, 'Could she do the same for them before she goes back over?' As they chatter on at her, a tiny woman struggles towards her under a white mountain of cloth.

'Here she is, Brigid,' Might-be-Marie says to the bride to be.

'Sure, isn't she a sight for sore eyes?' Brigid says. 'I'm so happy you could make it for me wedding, Barbara.'

Brigid – 'the best of the bunch' Seamus had told her on the way over – takes both of Barbara's hands and squeezes them tightly. She has a face covered in freckles and a huge, wide smile. She is half buried under a white lace dress with huge, lumpy bows. Her legs hang short and stout beneath stiff petticoats. Her head and arms poke out through more billowing waves of cloth, and she looks as if she is slipping right through the middle of it. The vast, weirdly starched veil is too much for her small head and arcs stiffly round her frizzy, pinned-down hair. The youngest-looking girl turns to Barbara, and says, 'Is she not a fairy tale princess?'

Though she tries to push the thought out of her mind, the veil reminds Barbara of a beekeeper's hat. She tells Brigid, 'You look lovely.'

Might-be-Marie beams along with the bride, and says, 'Ah, yer talk gorgeous, so you do.'

Barbara has been unable to pick out much of what has been said from all these mouths that set words off racing like horses. But she likes the up and down rhythms of these girls' chatter and she touches Might-be-Marie's face with her glove, and says, 'So do you.'

The crowd pile into the road and the procession moves to the church a half-mile along the Ballyrut road and Barbara settles, thankful, into the girls' warmth with their arms linked either side of hers as they follow the bride and groom along the rough, bubbled tarmac. The service is taken by the oldest priest she has ever seen, hobbling through the mass between two canes. His feeble voice struggles to reach her under the echo of shoe soles slapping on the stone floor as the altar boys rush around. They ring bells and swing incense, hold candles and crucifixes while he mumbles his prayers. They lift up the chalice and ciborium for his blessing as he quivers precariously between his sticks, and at the Communion they hold him up, their hands cupping each elbow and almost lifting him down to the altar rail. His hands are shakier than his speech, which forces the waiting mouths to make undignified snaps at the wafers like hungry dogs. Just as he reaches her, he stumbles and his knees creak and crack as he is righted by his young guards. She can't help wondering, as she watches him quivering, what they would do if he died before the wedding is done, and then has to hold back blasphemous laughter by biting hard on the inside of her lip. He rambles on a good long while after they're back in the seats, and with his low voice she hears nothing until the final round of 'amens' and it's over. She slips into the hurrying throng, but she erupts before she's properly outside and once she starts she can't stop. She laughs, gasps, laughs, wipes tears with a hanky fished out of her bag, laughs, smiles helplessly at the watching families. She apologises eventually, mostly in the direction of her fiancé's parents. The mother, 'Old Mother Ox' she says to herself, glares and says something to Seamus, who flushes but says nothing back.

As the collective male thirst increases, the men lead the way in the second holy procession of the day: to the pub. Seamus' father, separated from Old Mother Ox by the mother of the groom, pats the seat next to him. She sits where she is prompted, teary-eyed and coughing in the already thickening tobacco fug. He smiles and nods to her, and then chuckles as he hands her a half-glass of Guinness. 'Thanks, Tommy.' She feels that here at least a battle may be won, and sips gratefully at the bitter, thick black gunge. Seamus sits down heavily beside her, a pint in one hand, a whiskey in the other. All around her pints – halves, of course, for the women – are downed with speed. Cigarettes dangle from lips as more yarns are spun, more gossip swapped and gags shared. Voices call out for a bit of music. Guests just arrived are greeted with yells and cheers. People pass along drinks and drinks and drinks. The alcohol keeps coming, even for her, though she is struggling to get her first glass even half emptied. She has a collection of spirits and beers around her, all unasked for, which the teenage girls siphon off eagerly. Even they, between three to six years from being old enough to be in the pub under their own steam, are drinking her under the table. As the night goes on she has, finally, begun to tune in to what is being said. Out of the swift slur of their talk she picks up the gist, even making out complete sentences from time to time. Curses and swear words, having been swallowed back in the churchyard on account of the priest, make a break for it from all these wide-open traps: foul profanities and blasphemies bubble from all the mouths from the instant they get beside the bar.

Seamus' father, with a half-dozen drinks inside him, stands up, holding a glass to the low ceiling for a toast.

'To Brigid and Packie on the day of their wedding. Welcome Packie to the Duffys. And here's to our Brigid making a fine Fitzsimmons.' He smiles at the room, beer sloshing and spilling as his glass arcs through the air.

An ugly man with a big head, bigger ears and watery, almost clear-coloured eyes stands up. 'That's our Conor,' Seamus whispers to her. 'He climbed the ugly tree and then hit every fucking branch on the way down.' She almost chokes on her drink, giggling, though the joke is mean.

The ugly brother grins and shouts, 'To the poor ould groom, on the day of his doom!'

All the mouths open into big round holes and laughter crackles around the pub.

'And we all know the three rules of marriage. In the first year of marriage, Packie will yell and Brigid will listen. In the second year, Brigid will yell and Packie will listen. By the third year, they'll both be yelling and all the fecking neighbours will listen.'

The brother is pulled away amid the roar of applause, down the room to the bar. As if he were a hair plucked from a mole, another brother, the bald one, sprouts up in his place. He is, Barbara sees, even drunker than the ugly one.

'Here's to marriage, even them planning a heathen Brit marriage. I mean, by the almighty loving Jeysus, Seamus, you must have knowed it took us hun-de-reds of years to run de fuckers out, and here you are, single-fucking-handedly bringing them back.'

Laughter ripples and Seamus rises, bristling.

'I'm only joking yer. C'mon now. She's alright enough.' He bows before her and swings one arm. 'Us Fenians warmly welcome you to God's side of the sea.'

She thought the joke was funny but doesn't want to upset Seamus, who is only looking out for her. So she smiles and then looks away and down into her drink. His father pulls him back down into his seat saying, 'Never mind now,' and hands him a cigar. Seamus, mollified, sits and grins his big grin into all the faces, red with merriment and booze.

Baldy starts to sing a song at the top of his voice. It stops the nattering like a thrown bucket of cold water, and Brigid, whose day it should be, has lost the fleeting attention that she commanded for the first time in her life by getting married. As he sings, an army of Republican eyes are on the English woman, and many of those eyes are flecked with tiny glints of malice, like a hundred ice-blue torches. Barbara, the English woman, who is as near as damn it to beautiful and who has just reached for only her second drink of the night, tips her glass – a gin and tonic – and gulps down half of it in one go. She clears her throat and then her voice, that reaches high enough though it can't quite get to on-key, rises to join in with Baldy:

'And I'm off to join the IRA and I'm off tomorrow morn.
And we're all off to Dublin in the green, in the green
Where the helmets glisten in the sun
Where the bayonets flash and the rifles crash
To the echo of the Thompson gun.'

She shouts out I-R-A as if it is a football chant, the way she has heard it a dozen times or so on her trips with Seamus to the pubs down in Levenshulme (though never as far as Ancoats where he said he'd never take her because that's where the dregs do their drinking). The room cheers and claps and Baldy salutes her, and says, 'Good woman!'

Seamus beams and puts his arm around her as the band, finally arrived, begins a tune, though he still glances at Baldy from time to time and grips his knee with his free hand.

Brigid comes over and asks him will he dance with her. He follows his sister dutifully to the centre of the room, though the look on his face suggests he is being led to the stocks. Just as she reaches the tiny clear space in the floor there is a shout from behind the bar and a daft-faced puppy races out and jumps up at her, shoving its paws slap bang onto her dress. She squeals and jumps backwards and it jumps forwards. They repeat this a few times, as if she's decided to dance with the friendly mongrel instead, and the dress is soon decorated with mud smears across the skirt. Seamus pushes in front of her and the dog now tries to jump at him. It meets his boot and the air leaves its body in a rasp. It sits dazed on the floor and tries to move backwards out of the way, but it can't move fast enough for Seamus, who gives it a huge kick that flips it completely over. It is screaming and the sound fills the room as if they were not at a wedding after all but a funeral where a bereaved spouse has finally fathomed the permanence of death. The dog's front leg dangles and swings as it scrambles for escape, nails clicking and sliding on the wooden floor, eyes bulging, still shrieking, colliding with a stool as it tries to right itself and falling back down where, after a good long struggle, it stays. Seamus lifts his boot over the dog but Brigid pulls him backwards, almost toppling him in the process.

'Fer god's sake, it's done. Leave de ting alone now,' she says.

Barbara jumps out of her seat and pushes her way through the heap of bodies who, having jumped up to see what might happen, are already setting themselves back down on chairs.

'Do something,' she says, and looks around her, looks at him and his brothers, who are stood as calm as you like, drinks already once again in their hands.

'Somebody bloody do something!' She shoves a couple of people out of the way and reaches down to try and scoop the dog up.

'It'll bite yer, stupid,' Seamus says. But the dog does nothing of the sort – just trembles as it watches her approach.

'Then help me!' she shouts. Seamus looks at her for a minute or so, his face blank, before he smiles as if she were asking him to resuscitate a bug. Might-be-Marie slips beside her and bends down to the dog, feels along the leg, says, 'Jeysus, it's dis-ler-cated.' The father gets down on the floor beside her, and says, 'Hold it tight there.' There is a huge click and a single cry from the dog, and then it lifts itself clumsily up off the floor. Barbara tries to stroke the dog but it's already away, incredibly using all four legs, and makes its escape to the shelter of the rooms at the rear of the inn. She picks up a packet of cigarettes and matches off the nearest table and, though she doesn't smoke, gets one lit without asking who they belong to. She goes to the toilet, where a few puffs and the thought that won't let up – of Seamus kicking out like that and the poor creature's face looking up at them all – has her dizzy as hell. She throws the rest of the cigarette into the toilet bowl, sits herself down and puts her head in her hands. And she listens to the celebrations, hastily resumed, coming in at her through the walls.

Barbara tries to avoid the lumpy, sawdust-covered piles that sway dangerously under her raised heels as the boat swings with the sea, trying not to breathe in the stink as she moves towards the door leading to the deck. There is no need to be wide awake and worrying now she is heading back to England but she can't sleep even though she is irritable through weariness. So Seamus' mother doesn't like her, making a show of telling everyone she'd not be going to

Dublin to see them off 'on account of her legs'. She doesn't like her back. Same goes for Baldy and there's a couple of his sisters she'd like to give a good talking too as well. That's family for you. Seamus has been declaring his remorse all day, said his 'clattering' of the puppy was down to the drink heaped on him by everyone he said hello to, said she knows he's not a drinker and doesn't he always make sure he's in a decent state to get her home to her parents at a decent time. He looked at her with shiny eyes until she gave a thin smile and then bundled his coat into a pillow and fell asleep.

They had stopped by the cottage on the way back to say their goodbyes. Seamus' father and a heavily pregnant woman sat at a solid wood table that took over half the floor space. Seamus went to stand by his mother by the sink and together they overfilled the narrow space. Mother Ox stood with arms folded, watching her. The friendly sisters were all out in Dublin for the day. 'Looking for work,' Seamus' father said. Seamus' brothers were outside arguing over the extension being built on. Barbara stood by the door. With five bodies the kitchen was crammed. She couldn't for the life of her imagine how such a huge family could fit in – all squashed into this tiny place with just the three rooms. A kid in a filthy jumper came in the door, bawling, and the pregnant woman flicked a towel and shouted, 'OUT!' and the kid went back out again, bawling even louder. The ugly brother, Colin or Cormack or whoever he was, stuck his big square head through the open window, and yelled, 'Nola, where the hell's the hammer?'

The pregnant woman shrugged her shoulders at him and lit a cigarette.

'For fuck's sake,' he said, and disappeared again. Seamus laughed and went outside.

'I'm Nola,' she says to Barbara, and puts out a grubby hand with a big smile. 'I wasn't able to get to the wedding with the size of me.'

Another shout arrives at the window. 'Nola, did you see the fucking level?'

'No.'

'Merciful Jesus. If we were crucifying Christ, sure we'd never find the fucking nails in this hope-fucking-less house.'

A Jack Russell came sniffing up at Barbara and then ambled to the back door, where it scratched and whined.

'Get to yer bed,' Nola said, and pulled her heavy belly out of the chair. 'She can't go out, she's in heat,' she said.

Barbara spotted the little circles of blood marking its trail from range to chair to door. Nola put her foot on a grey rag under the chair and zig-zagged it over each dot of blood in turn.

Barbara blushed and lowered her head.

'Make way for the queen of Sheba,' the mother said, and snorted, then turned back to the sink and filled a kettle.

'Don't mind the begrudger,' Nola whispered to her, and pulled a face at the mother's back, 'sit yourself down.' She tilted a chair at Barbara and winked.

Nola flicked something black out of the sugar bowl, the ash from her cigarette settling in its place before pushing it, along with a mug of tea and a bottle of milk, to Barbara. And Barbara sat there, face burning, in the kitchen for a long, long while, until Seamus came back and said Joe was here and it was time to go.

Barbara stands at the rail and watches a band of gold glimmering over at the edge of the sea as the sun drags the morning up. The rain starts but she stays where she is, thankful to be on her way home. She's never thought of it raining at sea, though of course it must. The clouds drift everywhere, after all. The rain is hard and icy, raps her knuckles until they sting, which brings back memories of maths lessons and nuns with rulers. It hits her across the face again and again and drives her back inside, where she finds Seamus awake and talkative. She lets him drape his coat over her damp cardigan and nods and smiles, though she feels, suddenly, just like that strip of light she saw on the deck; a frail and faint illumination, half crushed under something huge and harsh and cold.

Barbara is shamed. She is lying on a hospital bed that smells of damp and blood. She can't bear to think that she herself smells the same way. The twins lie beside her in a cot, tiny packages of lacy blankets folded into a V at the bottom that remind her of the butcher's rectangles of wrapped meat. The babies were hammering at her for a day and a half as they fought their way out and she is sore and bruised and exhausted.

'Stupid. Stupid. Stupid,' she says to herself. She tries not to think about the night everything went wrong, when she was in Manchester with Seamus for the big dance at the Victoria. He had asked permission from her parents for her to stop over, assuring them that she'd be stopping with his sisters who were newly arrived in the city for work and she was so excited that they'd said yes, her first proper night away from home. She remembers the beauty of the dance hall; the grandness of the setting with the light through the huge stained-glass windows throwing dazzling peacock colours onto the wooden floor, the swirling frocks and the upright black lines of the suits, being hypnotised by the constant soft movement. And then the horrendous noise and crush in the pub in Salford after the dance, the insistence of his sisters on her having a drink, and then another. Though she had only a quarter of what was offered it was way too much and she had to be held up between Seamus and some friend of his on the way back. She remembers nothing of getting up the stairs past the landlady but can still hear the dull thwack as she fell on the mattress. She remembers the room spinning and his persistent whispering over and over that he loved her, that she belonged to him, as she fought off nausea and then that sudden colossal heavy weight as if she were being buried and a pain that the alcohol flattened and threw into the distance, and then nothing. When she woke in the morning, her legs were sticky and something felt lodged in her belly like a splinter. She remembers sobbing, and him holding her hand, and saying, 'I want only to marry you.' And when she pushed his hands away he stood beside her, a scowl on his face, letting her cry.

She hears the babies whimper and she struggles to believe that this is God's design for how babies come into the world. She had looked forward to the birth, not because of motherhood which she fears, but because the indignity of pregnancy would be over. She hated being so conspicuous in her proportions when she was towards the end of the nine months, hated the waddling around, barely able to bend herself to sit or stand. She felt clown-like and clumsy when trying to navigate spaces or getting wedged into whatever chair she sat in, of being unable to stop wind suddenly breaking, publicly and loudly, or her bladder leaking. When her waters broke and she was rolled into the ward and the nurse came in with the razor, she realised that the shame wasn't over. As the labour progressed, her sense of disbelief, like one more hard slap across the face, kept building as they wheeled her into a room and a doctor, a stranger, poked and prodded between her legs, talking all the while to the midwife as if he were inspecting some farm animal. She turned herself to the wall, blocked it all out, until the pain really began to hit and ripped her in two and she had no more thoughts. Now she is like a prisoner under guard, snared by a constant stream of people: nurses, midwife, medics, visitors, all standing round her bed and talking over her. And she dreads the daily doctors who bend down as they pull up her covers, pens clicking as they stare. The nurses speak in high voices to her. 'How are we?'

they sing-song. And when she says nothing, they sing even higher on her behalf, telling her, 'You're doing just fine.' She gets a half-dozen of these cheery, squeaky greetings every day, as if she were not newly a mother but another irritable infant to mollify. The babies are fed and full and sleeping. Her eyes close and open and close again as she fights fatigue. She feels the energy drain from her as if from a tap. She hears the click of heels, faint at first and then other footsteps join in and the rhythm brings to mind a tap-dancing routine from a Christmas show she saw as a child. As the steps continue, doctors and nurses are suddenly coming out of doorways and adding to the throng. And she wants to join in, but is left behind in her bed.

She is jolted by the scrape of a chair on the floor, opens wet eyes, screwed up against the light, and sees her mother and father. They are talking in low voices to each other, oblivious to her consciousness. The word 'fuck' jangles like a siren and when she realises she's thinking the word herself, it shocks her awake. Her father smiles and looks just past her head, holds up flowers for her to sniff at, and she heaves herself into a sitting position. She watches him put them down and pick up a baby from one of the cots. Her mother tidies the magazines on the bedside cabinet and takes the other baby. Barbara listens to their high-pitched cooing at the little meaty parcels and feels a rush of blood that heats her face. She whispers, 'Jesus,' and feels the urge to yell it, over and over – 'Jesus, Jesus, JEEE-SUS' – right into their beaming faces, to throw some of that shock onto them.

'How are you?' her mother says.

'I'm very tired,' she answers and hasn't any more to say, as if words, like babies, are something she has recently been emptied of, something she has pushed and pushed, until exhausted, to expel. She lies there without a single word more in her mind, listening to her parents chattering and the ward clock ticking. Seamus arrives and, as always, charms the matron into forgoing rules, letting him join the two allotted visitors around the bed. He has driven Barbara to distraction from the off, moving around the bed, lifting flowers and cards, and shouting his hellos at the other mothers or the nurses going past. He sits with her parents and takes the babies from them, one in each huge hand and looks at them as they fidget within their blankets. He smiles and looks just then, exactly like he did when they first met at the church dance, when his every word rolled as soft and fluid as they did across the dance floor, and when she last saw that same softness in those blue eyes of his. She hears one of the babies squall mildly and shuts her eyes against it. She feels strangely empty now nothing dances deep within her belly. For the past eight months it's fizzed and crackled as if she had fireworks in there. The midwife joked that her babies must have been boxing each other, trying to budge each other out of the way.

Her father is laughing with Seamus about something. He's fond of Seamus still, despite 'what they did', as he calls it, especially as Seamus came with her to tell her parents of what happened between them and of his honest intentions towards her. When her father started to shout, Seamus listened with his head down and then slid away from her off the couch and half knelt on the floor beside her father's chair. He looked, Barbara thought, ridiculous, as if he were asking her father and not her, to marry him. He grasped her father's hand and looked, first at him and then at her mother, with tears in his eyes as he tried to open the jewellery box he held in one hand.

'James, Grace, can you ever forgive me?' Barbara glanced at her parents who seemed transfixed with the clownish, kneeling penitent.

'Well, I've said my piece. We'll say no more about it.'

With that, her father's forgiveness, which is, after all, the only important forgiveness in the house, is granted. Her mother's forgiveness piggybacks that of her husband's, which leaves only Barbara to not forgive Seamus. She knows that he thinks he loves her, absolutely and always. He always clasps her hands in his and hugs her to him and tells her of his plans for them, for what they will have. What he is giving her is something distorted, it is not enough of what she needs and too much of everything she doesn't. She watches him now and remembers the red rose he brought her the first time he called to meet her parents, a love token framed in dark velvet that she put against her cheek before putting it into water where it stood straight and strong. After a day or so she noticed that the stem was becoming increasingly transparent until it revealed something crawling within. It was eaten away from the inside out until its stalk disintegrated and the leaves dropped, leaving a hunched and mottled skeleton behind. When she threw it away, it left a faint bad smell in her room. As Seamus gets to his feet and turns away from James and Grace, Barbara thinks she sees Seamus let a sneer bubble across his face that, when he sees her watching him, he pops with a sharp canine tooth. She looks at Seamus now and detests him for seeing her through what he needs, wants and feels, for seeing love as an invasion, a country to be conquered. She has been cheated all this while. He talked of love but like her father, he sees love as a matter of possession.

Her father hasn't said his piece. He has a lot more to say when Seamus isn't present. Barbara has come to dread spending time with him; he seems to have no end of barbed comments and a sermon ready every teatime.

'You're lucky Seamus is a good lad,' he keeps telling Barbara. She wants to scream at him that he's changed his mind all of a sudden, that it's a far cry from the time she brought Seamus to meet her parents and he smoked in their house without asking and James called him an 'Irish so-an-so' when he'd gone. She wants to ask what happened to his 'no good would come of marrying an Irish', to his insistence that she should take her pick from the local men at the church. She wants to remind him of all the times he complained of the influx of Irish, 'taking over the schools and churches', to ask him why he's refused point-blank to go to any Mass that Father Quinn took. Seamus has transformed into a hard-working, god-fearing man and all it took was a sliver of yellow metal. Barbara tried, once, to speak to Grace about what had happened to her, but the only thing she understood from her mother's whispered words, as she stood there red-faced and looking away from her daughter, is that men have it in them to be more physical and that he is putting things right now. She understands too that Seamus has been pardoned, that a wedding ring is all the punishment he will have for what he did. It is her, whose intentions nobody has ever asked about and for whom all the possibilities of what she might do in this life are now tiny lights in the back of her mind and fading daily, that has borne the brunt of her father's contempt in the run up to the wedding.

It was supposed to be the happiest day of her life. She went with her mother for her wedding dress fabric, to Kendal's in Manchester, for the good stuff. Her mother spent a fortnight on the dress, working all day and then up all hours as well, eyes bloodshot, index finger blood blistered, making something so special that no one could think the marriage was rushed through. It is taken from a Vogue pattern no less, and Barbara is trying on the almost-finished creation in the front room as her mother checks it front and back. It is long of sleeve, full of skirt, and her mother ignored the pattern's v-neckline, horizontally banding the bodice to match the waist, therefore making it minus any hint of the advertised cleavage. A double row of taupe daisies, running perfectly uniformly across the top band of the bodice, lift it out of the realm of homemade and give it an unlikely air of city couture. Her father comes in as she walks to and fro in front of the mirror above the sideboard, swinging the skirt with her hands, smiling for the first time in months at her reflection. He looks Barbara up and down.

'It's too clingy is that for my liking.'

'Don't you be so daft,' her mother says.

'It's not right – will you look at her?'

'Give over. It's a lovely style,' her mother says at last, as her disappointed fingers run over the stitching along the rim of the skirt where it rises over the slight puff of her stomach.

'She doesn't look decent.'

Barbara colours, stung and angry, bites her lip and looks at her feet. She wishes her mother would say something, stand up to him, but she knows she won't and she stands there on the rug fighting back tears.

'I'm not having it. We'll have the whole parish thinking she's a trollop.'

'It's fine. Would you have her going down the aisle in a dress as loose as a circus top? They'd soon talk then.'

'If she'd kept herself bloody proper, we'd not have to worry about that.'

'I won't have you swearing in this house.'

Message delivered, he sits down in his armchair and snaps opens his paper. Her mother's mild words have shown that, on the matter of the dress, she is putting her foot down but the damage is done, Barbara's skin prickles and burns. She helps her mother repack the sewing box, steps out of her heels and scoops them into her fingers. Her father doesn't look up as they file silently out of the room.

'Here's Pamela,' her father says now, and Barbara turns her head and watches her sister, just off the bus from Rochdale, stride down the ward. Pamela says hello and leans in to give Barbara a kiss. Barbara means only to return that light kiss, to ask her sister how she's enjoying being free of school, how she's finding the new factory, but yet she can't let go and clings on, as if she might absorb some of her sister's calmness through the skin. She begins to cry and Pamela hugs her.

'Nothing to worry about,' a nurse says cheerily. 'Just hormones.' Even with her face buried into her sister's coat, she can see clear as day the look her father will be sporting.

She can see his face, thin and slightly shiny; can see him kneading his cap with his fingers and casting sideways glances to see if people round the other beds are looking. And they will be. She is listening to herself wailing, and even though she wants it to stop it does the very opposite, keeps building and building. Two nurses come running and prise her away from Pamela, unhook her fingers from her sister's coat. One tells her, 'Enough now, Mrs Duffy,' and hearing her new name makes her scream. She keeps screaming until the injection is given and then a few seconds later she stops, as if a switch has been flicked, and slumps down upon the pillow. Her mother leans into her and puts a hand upon her shoulder, and says, 'Please, love.'

Barbara looks up at her. 'I want to go back,' she says.

'What?' her mother asks.

'I have to get back... to before.'

'Hush,' her mother says, and sits down on the bed. She pulls Barbara into her arms until her breathing levels out. Barbara feels like she is one of these babies strewn across the ward, needing to hold onto the comfort of a mother. She feels her heart beating, and its rhythm, thump-thump-thumping away, makes her feel that she is being controlled from the inside out. You don't live life, she thinks, life lives you. It's been grinding her deeper into a rut, even as she's gone to church, studied, taken all those tests. She's nothing now but a receptacle for her husband to empty himself into or babies to be pulled out of. She is a fish on a line – a lifeline – she thinks, and laughs out loud only minutes after stopping crying, which makes her mother look at her sharply. Barbara imagines having just enough energy to drag herself right out of the bed, to rise and get past them. Even as she sinks further into sleep amidst the clammy sheets, she sees herself moving into the light, leaving them all talking about grapes and slippers and water jugs as she heads into that blinding freedom she sees streaming through the windows every time she opens her eyes.

Barbara's tablets have made everything fuzzy. They've rubbed out the nightmares, bleached through the dark thoughts, smoothed the panicky episodes, blunted that ragged pain that pulsed with every heartbeat. But they have left her confused. Memories slip through her mind's fingers like the greasy dinner plates that have of late jumped from her hands when she's washing up, smashing themselves around her feet. 'Out of kilter,' the doctor told her. He said it would right itself in the end, once she was settled with her new babies, yet here she is, still swallowing these little green capsules daily. She has been a long while calm, no more hysterics, but still there remains a vague apprehension that pricks at her that there is something she should be remembering. They have also blurred time. Events have fused themselves to dates and days that she thinks they might not actually belong to. She feels at times as though she is in one of those speeded-up films, sidestepping unseen dangers hurtling towards her on all sides, has a sense of time flying past. So much time has slipped past her and she has no idea of where it's hiding. She ran into an old school friend at church last week. The woman – whose name has already sunk back into the depths of her permanently dozing memory – told her she was back from Canada where she had emigrated to, for some reason that Barbara can no longer recall and then asked her how long she had been married.

'Oh. Well. Years,' she had said, and slid her lips sideways, showing her neat teeth as she tried to pass it off as a joke, unable for the life of her to remember how many years since she'd been fastened to Seamus. And when she was asked the age of the twins she said, automatically, 'Two and a half,' and then wondered if that were the case, if they could already be that old, that big, and if so, why could she not recall their current faces. The only clear thought she had formed was that Canada must be a foreign-looking place. She is regarded, she knows, as a very lucky woman. Her parents, Pammy, the woman next door – whose husband can be seen with his arm round a certain Rochdale barmaid every Friday and Saturday night – they are always telling her so. Seamus is a hard worker, a good provider and he is still as proud as punch about them being married, his head rises to catch the looks they get when they are outside together. Since the boys were born he takes himself to the pub only on special occasions, likewise the bookies or the football. Seamus won't waste any money he doesn't have to. He is always counting, arranging notes and coins in piles on the kitchen table, divvying up how much is needed for this and that. They are one of only two families on the newly built council estate with a mortgage rather than a rent card. There is always money for food and the bills. They don't have to scrimp and save, like some. She is never without lipstick, can afford a trip every so often to the hairdressers. He likes them to be well dressed; 'a striking couple,' people say as they walk past in their Sunday best, the twins in matching outfits, trotting in front of them in shiny shoes like little black beetles. He's well in with the boss at the factory, he has a smile and a joke for everyone and they can't get enough of that voice of his, rising and falling like a stream splashing over a stone. Barbara has seen the effect he's had on more than a few women, recognises the way they lean at him when he speaks, how they stare at him when that flick of dark hair falls in front of his big blue eyes. If he sees it, he never responds, simply sails through them like a ship heading for port where he's putting his stamp on everything, painting rooms and tiling the bathroom or hard at it in the large garden that surrounds their corner house on three sides. He never stops. He's creosoted the fence that now clearly marks his territory in shining mahogany, dug over the bottom garden for potatoes and put in an iron gate in the six months since they moved in. He told her yesterday that he has picked out the colour for the front and back doors which he'll do once he's finished the path of yellow and white flagstones that he's weaving from the front door through the patches of pansies and the rose bushes to the gate.

She is glad to have moved on from their first cottage with the steep hill right outside the back door that sucked all the light out of the kitchen and looked like an animal waiting to pounce whenever she had to use the cold outside lavatory before sleeping. She is now only a few streets away from her mum and sister, though they call round to her far more than she calls round to them. She has taken to avoiding her father, whose raspy voice sets her teeth on edge. Seamus treads the same path as three-quarters or so of the people on the estate, a ten-minute walk to work that is housed, like a hermit crab, in the shell of the old cotton Mill. He has been promoted already to dispatch and counts out the orders as the trucks roll up. He's also landed the late evening security shift, walking home with the loading bay door key jangling with the others on his belt. He goes with her and the boys to church on a Sunday, taking her arm and linking it to his as they follow the boys skipping along either side of their aunty Pammy with James and Grace leading the way. Yes, she is lucky, to these half-blinded people to whom it would never occur to try and look below what glistens on the surface.

Seamus isn't the same indoors, he can hang up his cheery façade with his overall if he so chooses. He can march up the path waving and grinning at whoever he's walked home with only to let his smile fall off his face the minute the door is closed. He throws his dirty socks onto the end of the sofa and sits in his chair breaking wind as he mutters about the 'bloody Brit bastards' who, he declares, all have it coming to them. He scorns them for being tenants, for calling him Paddy or Mick or Murphy and yet they can't get a proper toehold in their own arse-end of a country while he's getting ahead alright. He will make a target of anything, mocks physical disability or people without much going on upstairs; he laughs at unfortunate personal circumstances or bad luck. Barbara keeps a mental list of people she knows only as cripple, hair lipped, specky, spotty, cross-eyed, humpbacked, retarded, cretin, pauper, gobshite, bastard, moron. She has forgotten so many more. He turns on her and the boys too. He came home yesterday after a double shift to find her reading in the kitchen and asked if she had enjoyed her day doing goddamn nothing except sitting on her fat arse. She was stung but said nothing, put his food on the table and went to sit by him. He took a taste of her casserole and said the tinkers back home did a better job of it with only a bonfire to cook on. She had yelled at him to sod off back to his greasy landlady stews if that was how he bloody well felt and he asked her where her sense of humour had got to as she ran upstairs. When Grace called round this morning, Barbara tried to tell her about it all, his insults and coarse language and the way he liked to try and poke her in the belly with the stiffened rabbits he brought home from hunting, despite her screaming at him to stop, before throwing them down on the table without a scrap of paper to catch the blood. Grace told her not to worry, that men can be downright insensitive when they were tired. She put a hand on Barbara's shoulder and smiled, said that someone had to be able to bring home the meat, if it was left to women like herself and Barbara, soft souls that they were, the whole family would starve. Barbara shrugged her off, groped for words to let her mother really see how it is something more, something rotten, festering. She thinks back to the fancy dress parade last week at the church. She had the boys model the cowboy costumes Grace had made them.

'Look, Seamus. Don't they look lovely?' He looked them up and down and then bent down from his chair and looked into their happy faces.

'You look bloody ugly.' He laughed and she watched, helpless, as they began to cry.

'You're a nasty piece of work,' she said as she grabbed the twins' hands and led them to the front door to wait for their aunty Pammy and Granny. Even when they came home with a huge pile of colouring books and crayons and the first-prize rosettes pinned to their shirts, they still wore those hurt expressions and tear streaks down their faces.

'I was only joking,' he said, 'your lot are too soft. You'll make bloody nancy boys of them.'

She said nothing to him at all. She let the boys eat crisps and wagon wheels before putting them to bed and she stayed upstairs reading a book, leaving Seamus to cook his own tea. It is the same when he hits them.

'It's doing no harm,' he says.

'They're bloody toddlers. They're far too small to be hit all the time. You only need to say something to them,' she says.

'Like you'd know. I've seen you telling them off – one stern word from you and they carry on doing whatever they like. Stop bloody interfering. It's only a clip round the ear,' he says.

Barbara sees his big hand ready for all this clipping. It is almost the size of their little heads and when she sees it being wielded like a paddle she puts herself between Seamus and whichever boy he's got at.

'You've got a bloody answer for everything,' she says.

'I've a right to learn my sons what to do,' Seamus tells her.

'They don't even bloody know what they've done wrong,' she says, struggling not to add 'It's *teach* you stupid fool'. She takes the boys into the kitchen, out of his way. And the smacks keep coming. If they bicker over a toy or say they don't want to finish their tea, if they leave the door ajar when they come into the front room or they are caught sneaking titbits to the new dog that he has told them isn't a pet. The boys are wary of him. They are more and more withdrawn when he's in the house. They sit as close to each other as they can get, whispering together instead of talking, closing down to silence whenever Seamus is anywhere near. With each cuff and slap, they bend their bodies further when they walk around him, looking like tiny, stooped old men as they toddle their way around the room. He came in once complaining about the name callers at work and she asked him why he didn't say something to the boss. He stared at her like she was an idiot, his lips drawn back as if he would bite her.

'Get to fuck,' he said.

There are stretches of time where he is almost the same inside as out. At such times he still smiles at her and even takes her hand sometimes and strokes her wedding ring, and then gently pinches her fingers and she remembers that same soft pinching the night they met, sees the man she almost fell for, sees that he thinks he is loving her and why she once believed she would learn to love him. At such times, when he breaks wind or curses in front of the boys and she tells him not to be so coarse, he'll say 'pardon my French' and do a little bow in front of her and she and the boys give little laughs. Days will pass, weeks sometimes, without a cross word from him, when his hands are meek and he's as playful as a puppy, when he pulls the twins close and tickles them until they cry. The time stretches long enough for her to stop thinking about what might set him off, for the boys to forget not to scatter their toys or keep their voices down. But then he'll snap and he's suddenly furious, the cause invisible, and the boys shrink back from him like plastic in front of the fire and she feels her heart oscillate like she's being pinched somewhere inside. She wanted to explain all this to her mother but the medication has poked holes in her memory. She has thoughts about intent and damage but no matter how much she tries to hold on to them, they fall through her sievelike brain and land in a dark heap God knows where. It is the way he does these things, the specific language used, the expression worn, the tone in his voice. It is the way he can turn in an instant. She remembers the festival-goers she saw on a BBC programme recently, somewhere in Italy she thinks. They wear masks on both the front and the back of their heads and the front one is normal looking but the other side is distorted, twisted, frightening. They could have modelled those expressions on Seamus. She knows she can't explain this to Grace so she keeps it inside herself. She goes about her daily business but finds those jeering faces floating in her mind's eye. 'Go away,' she says to herself as she washes up or pegs the washing out. Then she finds herself thinking over and over, The devil is in the details, and feels like her brain is crumbling into dust inside her skull.

Outside, Seamus jokes and slaps backs and shakes hands. He keeps smiling even when ignorant mouths hurl casual insults, acting as if all of that is water off a duck's back. He is large and loud and always laughing. Inside, Seamus is whoever he wants to be, whatever suits him. He could come home tonight swearing or singing, arms open or fists clenched. He could talk to her and the boys or he could walk straight past them and be silent most of the night. As he's started saying of late, it's his fucking house. Lucky Barbara, she thinks a lot, these days, and smiles, with the kind of smile a condemned woman might wear, when she is sick of crying. Her home is a battlefield. There is no refuge. Jamie and Tommo are forever shouting for her, telling her some story that doesn't make it up the slippery slopes of her mind, their high voices like little pins constantly pricking. At night she enters another, secret combat zone that she cannot bring herself to talk about, not even with Pammy. Seamus is forever pawing at her in the dark, knocking against her skin with his knees and knuckles as she pushes him back towards his side of the bed. If she manages to fight him off, she falls asleep drained, and if he gets his way, as is the usual result, she remains awake long after him and gets up shattered. Now the boys tiptoe around at home, unsure of Seamus who blows hot and cold with them, play-fighting one minute, snarling the next. And she makes very little noise. She does her utmost to protect his sensitive ears from the noise of his children or the soft clanging of pots on the cooker. Aside from that there is only the turning of a page of a magazine or a book, or, when she is in the same room as her husband of an evening, the slight rustle of her skirt against her tights as she draws her knees up under her until she is a compact little parcel on the sofa. It has been this way for so long that she has squashed the good times, the happy memories into the space of a single day though she knows it is her drugged-up memory playing tricks again; she doesn't think the days she's felt happy would stretch into a whole year but there must surely have been months. She sighs the way she's learned to, on the inhale of breath. Seamus doesn't notice this, it doesn't disturb him. Her sighs, like her thoughts, are soundless.

◌

The return to Ireland that she had dreaded for days, in that detached, slightly unreal way that the tablets allow her, is almost over already. Barbara had expected to run into at least a few of Seamus' brothers and sisters on the boat to Dublin; when the letter arrived announcing that his father was gravely ill, Seamus had rushed over to Salford where many of his brothers and sisters now live, to distribute travel fare and make sure that they could all get back. Knowing that her almighty row with Old Mother Ox had done the rounds, Barbara had prepared herself for the frosty reception, only to have the anti-climax of the largely empty ferry. She had come so she could pay her respects to Tommy. Seamus' father was the only one, aside from Brigid, who had behaved decently to her. Brigid is the only one of them Barbara has had contact with for – she counts on her fingers – almost four years, since her first miscarriage. It is enough; the girl has enough heart for the whole lot of them. When the twins were not quite three, Barbara's belly swelled again, only to have a perfect-looking, stillborn boy laid out after six months. By the time Barbara got out of the hospital, Brigid had packed in her maid's job and was by her side to lend a hand. Grace was also calling round each morning to see to the boys and Pamela took a turn every evening. Since the burial, whenever Barbara wakened, one of them would be at the bedside, ready to hold her hands as she lay there as still as a corpse, softly persuading her to try and get up and dressed. Old Mother Ox, who was over on a visit, turned up with Orlaigh in tow.

Pamela brought them into the bedroom and went downstairs to make a pot of tea and the three of them sat there in silence listening to Pammy crying in the kitchen where she thought she was being discreet. Old Mother Ox sat herself down.

'I never lost a baby,' she said. And sat there, satisfied, with her arms folded and the chair creaking under her mass.

Orlaigh stood there open-mouthed. 'Mammy!' she said.

Barbara swung her legs slowly over the side of the bed and yanked the door open.

'Take this bitch away from me before I swing for her.'

Orlaigh had dragged her mother out of the room and as they waddled downstairs, Barbara yelled.

'You're a wicked, fat old cow. Get out of my house before I fucking throw you out.'

Brigid had come running, pushing past them on the stairs and hugged her tight.

'Go on. Get out. You old bitch,' she kept saying.

They were long gone by the time Seamus was home from work and nothing was said to him about their visit. Barbara stayed out of bed after that, gaunt and mute and jumpy, spreading her sorrow around the house like a gas. Brigid stayed another week, always nearby but never in the way, helping Pammy with a bit of housework or doubling up with Grace to wash the clothes. Brigid put a plate of food in front of Seamus when he got in of an evening. She made a real fuss of the boys, played games to stop them getting bored and gave them too many sweets. They loved her fiercely even though they complained that she was squishing them whenever she grabbed them for a cuddle. Brigid stayed until Barbara joined her one time at the sink and helped her dry the dishes. She had left the weekend after, teary-eyed as she made her goodbyes and headed off for the bus back to Manchester, making Barbara promise to eat. Her letters arrived every month or so after that, a sprawl of clumsy lettering and badly spelled sentences, starting and ending with *my dear sister* and a muddle of incomprehensible half-told stories in the middle. The latest letter made Barbara smile despite herself, but it was short lived; Seamus took it as a sign. The smile sunk under their old familiar wrangle as she tried to stop him clambering upon her, rolling this way and that like a heavy rock, until she could barely breathe.

Barbara and Seamus are staying again with the McGinnises. Before Conor had even time to take their bags at the port, Brigid came to her rescue one more. She stood in front of Seamus and told him firmly that there wasn't the room for everyone at Mammy's house and that she'd already sorted a place for him and Barbara and the twins. Brigid the Buffer, she thinks now, but gratefully so. Being shut up in that cramped little space with Old Mother Ox doesn't bear thinking about. The thought is enough to send a jolt of alarm thrusting through her damped-down nerves. Even yesterday, when everyone was squashed together at the cottage waiting for the men to load the coffin onto the hearse outside and the time was ripe for appeasement, Old Mother Ox had made a meal of her being there, moving herself right up against the wall opposite where Barbara was standing and then declaring over all attempts to shush her that the day was ruined. Still, she is glad she could say her goodbyes to Seamus' father. She tries to picture his face and gets only a hazy outline of features, though she hears his voice distinctly; kind words float in her memory along with the ends of anecdotes. With Tommy gone, she feels more unprotected somehow, a lost dog surrounded by a strange, hostile pack. She senses also a threat of some future onslaught; imagines them marching en masse down the hill to take over her home. So she is glad of the pills. They have pulled off their magician's trick perfectly, again, and sped up time while she's been here. The priest, she was amazed to see, was still going, though he was transported this time, by his altar boys, to the bench at the side of the altar to watch a younger priest do his stuff. She seems to have lived most of her life in one fucking church or another. She is swearing again. She finds it funny that the one thing her mind is sharper than ever at is swearing. What she never says out loud she makes up for in every thought. As she packs the suitcase she wonders what her mother, who crosses herself after saying 'damn and blast it', would make of her new found predilection for foul language.

The funeral is done and dusted and tonight she and the boys will be on their way back to England, where they all belong. Only three hours to go. Her hands move over her stomach, which is fizzling again. She feels the scald as heartburn sends acid gurgling into her throat. Only six months since her second miscarriage, mercifully early on that time, and another is already forming, will soon be filling her insides again. She can hear the boys outside, their excited shouts high-pitched and girlish. She looks through the window to watch them run around, feels glad that they can let off steam, tries to remember what it is like to run with bare legs through wet grass. She goes to the door to call them in for their dinner and sees they've gone round the back of the house. As she walks round she hears the dog barking. She turns the corner and sees the boys running, as they've done every day, to Joe who is taking out the food for the dog. She hears Jamie pleading, 'Mr McGinnis, can we touch him now?' and sees the poor dog straining and straining, hanging, half choked, and coughing at the end of its chain. The day they landed, she asked Joe if he would let it run around with the boys for a while and he said in his friendly way, 'I don't think so Barbara. If he ran away into the farmer's field it'd be curtains for him.'

Her stomach flips and she feels bilious. She wonders whether this baby will survive. Pammy and Grace would be over the moon if she had a girl. Amanda May, she thinks – if it does, if it is. She cringes as she hears the dog's hysterical yelping, the clanking of its chain as it slobbers over the twins. She can't bear to look at that dog with its big wet eyes watching her every move as if begging her to let it go. Perhaps a quick end from the farmer's gun would be better for that poor beast, if it came after a taste of freedom. Her own manacles are noiseless, but for all the difference it makes they might as well clang like church bells whenever she moves. She also has a life that can be measured in yards.

‘My trousers are too fucking tight,’ he says, and marches up the stairs and then bangs around in the bedroom before coming down in a different shirt. He tucks the shirt into his trousers and she sees the belt buckle digging into his belly.

‘I’m not in the fucking mood for this, not at all,’ he says, and sits at the table with his tea and his paper. No, she thinks, and neither am I.

She hears the commotion from the front room and goes in. The twins have somehow managed to get the baby out of her pram and are squabbling over whose lap she should sit on, stroking at her with clumsy, grubby paws.

‘That’s enough,’ she says, and picks Amanda out of Jamie’s lap before the christening gown gets dirty, holding the laughing baby to her chest as she walks back into the kitchen. She wraps a towel around the baby to protect her dress and undoes her blouse, wedging the edge of the towel underneath her breast. Amanda starts to feed but every so often she stops and looks all around her and then up at her mother, arms reaching up to her, before starting again. She has always been the same, Barbara thinks, letting us know she’s here and not wanting to miss a trick. She came out bawling, having been finally turned in the womb. Barbara imagined the baby breaching herself on purpose, wedging herself firmly in, having heard the chaos outside for the past nine months.

‘No need to check her lungs,’ the midwife said, laughing as she cleaned her, still screeching like a banshee. When the midwife handed her over, Barbara tucked her into the crook of her arm and lay in the bed, eyeball to eyeball with her new daughter, whose tiny face was scarlet and furious and screwed up so tight she looked like a wrinkly old apple, desperate to feel that skin, warm with life, nestling against her again. She heard her mum and dad whispering to Seamus to let her be, that she'd loosen her grip when she knew it was staying, and she felt fear jab its fingers along her spine and she clutched her daughter then, as tightly as her daughter clung to her. Seamus liked to pick her up when she was sleeping, ignoring Barbara's plea, lifting her up high, putting his nose into her soft belly. But she began to make too much noise for his liking, not waking peacefully like the twins, but bursting into tears as soon as her eyes were open, letting rip with her little lungs until she was picked up, her cry shrill and piercing as an air-raid siren. And now, at six months old, she refuses point-blank to be ignored. She can twist her body like a snake, always turning herself round to see who is coming and going. If they put her in her playpen she pulls herself vertical and waves at everyone. If that doesn't work, she screams with tears filling her big blue eyes until someone gives in to those stretched-out arms. Plumped and pink with her mother's milk and a smile that could melt stones, she bends them all to her will – except for Seamus. Sometimes he sticks his head right inside her pen and yells at her but she doesn't cower. She yells right back. They go head to head, each making their own animal noise until Barbara rushes in to get her out of his way. One time he yanked her up and she went rigid in his arms and screamed the place down until Barbara pulled her back off him. Though Seamus' bellowing is enough to have the boys quaking, the baby just keeps screaming right through it, in the end driving him, cursing, out of the room. When anyone else puts their face close to hers, she rewards them with a big smile and they are captivated by her, by those two blue marbles that look as if they are lighted from within.

Seamus comes back into the kitchen with his jacket balled up in his hand. He throws the jacket onto the table, half covering Amanda's head.

'Jesus, just look at it, like a little pig on yer tit,' he says.

'Do you have to be so crude?'

As she struggles to balance the baby and stand at the same time, she glances at the window and sees the familiar lump of bodies marching down the avenue.

'Oh, I don't bloody believe this,' she yells. She bangs the kettle down hard, which sets the baby off wailing and makes Seamus look up and glare.

'What?' he says.

'Here's the bloody circus,' she says. 'Only Brigid and Conor were supposed to know. What are they doing here, today of all days?'

'I've said nothing.'

'Your lot must communicate with bloody smoke signals then.'

She spits out the words like they are wasps trapped in her mouth and sends them buzzing around his ears. He grabs her by the shoulder but she hisses, 'Oh no you don't, not today,' and pushes him away. He lets her go as the gate clinks open. They come barging in, talking ten to the dozen, Conor prattling with Sean about football, Orlaigh with that smirk that Barbara has more than once felt like knocking off her face. She hasn't seen hide nor hair of them in well over a year and couldn't care less if she never set eyes on them again. The very sight of Old Mother Ox is a red rag to a bull where Barbara is concerned. Old Mother Ox nods at her and pushes out a distracted hello as she looks around for things to find fault with later. Brigid materialises around the side of her mother and Barbara thanks the Lord that it's not Marie to contend with as well; the once-friendly girl who has grown into another dropper of sly insults while her voice, like a foghorn, carries her rough-cut words to the furthest corners of a room.

'How are you?' Barbara says, and kisses her.

Brigid gives Barbara a white teddy bear with a pink ribbon around its neck and holds her arms out to the baby, who is still sniffling. The baby looks uncertain but stretches out her chubby arms anyway, and Brigid sits her on her hip and then puts one arm around Barbara.

'I'm fine, so.'

Barbara reaches for the baby but Brigid gently pushes her away. 'Get yourself ready. I have her safe here now.'

Barbara feels anger ebb and flow as she puts the lipstick on in front of the dressing table mirror, colouring her lips as thick as all the bad blood. All initial diplomacy has long since dried up but as far as Old Mother Ox is concerned, any result of that is hard to detect. She goes back into the kitchen, smoothing down her dress. Used strictly for special occasions, it looks new. And it still fits her. Unlike her mother-in-law, the filling and emptying of her womb hasn't bloated her as yet; she puts her hands on her trim hips and looks Old Mother Ox right in the eye, wants her to see her at her best.

Orlaigh is rifling through the cupboards, looking for sugar and signs of dirt while his mother just sits there like she owns the place. Conor has found Seamus' new shotgun in the pantry and has it on his shoulder, looking down its sights.

'A grand day for rabbiting,' he says.

'Huh,' Barbara says.

Trust you to remind him of what he's missing, she thinks, and helps herself to a cup of tea from the pot. She pours a cup for Brigid without offering the rest of his lot anything. Conor drops the gun onto the floor and the loud clack of the barrel on the stone tile makes everyone jump. Seamus and Barbara, standing at opposite ends of the kitchen, look up at the same time and face one another as if they were going to the gallows rather than a christening. Conor picks up the gun and stands by the sink looking from one to the other. Seamus' anger narrows his eyes to slits.

Look at us, she thinks, the good, the bad and the bloody ugly. She is a character in a farce, only she can't walk off stage. So she takes her tea and walks out of the kitchen instead, motioning for Brigid to come with her, and leaves them to it while she goes to finish getting the boys ready.

Father Quinn greets them by the church door. Barbara digs her nails into her palms and twists her lips into the closest thing she has for a smile for him; him with his little visits to the house, the whole street knowing and no doubt gossiping, that he was there for the 'marital issues'. Walking in, that first time, after a single knock like he'd known them all their lives with his cheery 'How' yer?' making her first think that he was another of Seamus' brothers. He didn't give her the chance to offer but asked her to put the kettle on before sitting himself down in Seamus' hastily vacated chair. He came weekly to sit with Seamus, muted voices and laughter coming through the wall. When Seamus bought the record player, she sat in the kitchen listening to Father Quinn singing along to The Dubliners, dumbfounded to hear a priest singing bawdy tunes. And every week, as they took their seats in the front room, after providing a pot of tea she was banished to the kitchen bench, reading. She was startled when the priest finally came directly into the kitchen, sat down at the table and put his fedora on top of her magazine. Seamus made himself scarce, took the spade and rake out of the pantry and headed out to the back garden. Barbara made another pot of tea.

'How are you, Mrs Duffy?'

'Okay,' she said.

'How are the boys?'

She is still thinking of how to answer that when another question comes.

'You know, it's not always easy for the likes of us. There are some who don't make us welcome in this fine country of yours. That said, Seamus knows full well now, he must curb that temper of his. And I told him to pay more attention to his beautiful wife. He smiles broadly at her and rises to leave.

'I'm sure that will sort it out then.' Her words are sharp as knives.

Father Quinn's eyebrows furrow the same way Seamus' do and he looks angry. He nods his head, finds his smile again and when he speaks his voice is still soft.

'Would you like me to find someone for you to talk to? At St Vincent's?'

'Ah, of course,' she replies. 'It's the nuns for me. No thanks.'

Father Quinn looks at her as she stands up.

'We all suffer, Mrs Duffy.'

She thinks of Jamie upstairs in bed, who after dropping his cup into his dinner the other night, sports two thick, red welts that run vertically up his skinny chest like a pair of braces. She stares at the priest for a good while and then hands him his hat. She is still standing there after he's walked out the gate and Seamus has come back in. He looks at her for just a second, then lowers his eyes.

'Shall we ask your mother to babysit tonight?' he says, sheepishly. 'Get ourselves to the Crown?'

And she feels that same bitterness sting, that her own mother would go chasing, behind her back, for the priest before trying to talk to her. Her mother did it gently but she ambushed her all the same, with her hushed talk of duty. She can't look at her without feeling betrayed. It's enough to get through the day without falling asleep. She hasn't the energy to rifle through her closet for a dress. And she doesn't want her mother here, not today, with Father Quinn's smugness still fizzing in her guts.

'I have a headache,' she says, 'you go on down.'

'Father Brierley is ill today,' Father Quinn says, and looks around at them each in turn.

58

'I'm afraid I'll have to do.'

As he fully expects, Seamus' family give out a chorus of 'That's grand, Father' and they crowd round to shake his Dubliner hand. Barbara says nothing at all to him but waits until he has taken his leave to dress for the service, waits until the last smoker has climbed back up the steps from the main road and gone inside before rousing herself to do likewise.

She watches them as she walks down the aisle, noisy even when whispering as they settle themselves into their seats among the regular congregation. She watches Old Mother Ox try to make the boys sit beside her, muttering at Seamus to tell them to behave. Seamus is too distracted as he gets up out of his seat and Barbara smiles to see them wriggle out of her grip and go to sit in between Grace and James, who wrap arms round each one as they leaf through their hymn books. The altar boys steer Father Quinn right up to the altar before she reaches Pamela and sits beside her and the baby. And from there on in it is a long blurry hum of words that stretch on and on until she slouches in the pew. Even the hardness of the wood grating into her back fails to stop her eyes closing so she doesn't hear the cue, just feels her sister's fingers digging into her side.

Father Quinn is walking past them on his way to the font. Barbara and Seamus rise from opposite sides of the church and walk the godparents, Pammy and Conor, up to join him. Seamus takes the baby. Amanda May looks directly back at him and her smile suddenly fades, like the sun slipping behind a cloud, and she starts mewling. Father Quinn reaches over with the water and when Seamus bends her head over the font she gets lost in the folded depths of the gown. The satin slides down his palms and he grabs at her, which makes her howl. Pamela quickly reaches out and Seamus bundles the squirming baby awkwardly into her arms, where she pushes her tiny frame upright and looks round, smiling, as if she's pulled off a great trick.

Pamela lowers her gently over the font and Father Quinn dribbles water. Amanda May doesn't cry one bit; only fixes those two blue lasers on him and wobbles her fat little fist in his face.

Part Three
Love

Hello again. You should get a life. Why am I crying? No reason. Well, that's them – me mum and dad. Mummy and Daddy, Mother and Father, Mater and Pater. What a joke. We might as well have been raised by fucking wolves. 'Pops' our Jamie used to call him, because it annoyed him just enough to piss him off without getting belted, most of the time. And we'd call her 'Mammy' like the Irish did and she'd go apeshit. But we weren't scared of her. We'd sit there saying 'Mammy, mammy, mammy' as she brandished her slipper that was, compared to Dad's boots, as soft as a baby's fart. Even if she went berserk and started whacking us with it as fast as she could we'd be egging her on, from when she started to when she stopped. I sometimes wonder what might have happened all those nights ago at that dance if she'd not seen Dad. What if some local boy had stepped in front of Dad before he got to her, or if she'd lowered her head to discretely pick a bit of dinner from her teeth just as he reached her? Maybe Dad, with his pride dented, would have fucked off and asked another girl to dance. But she didn't and so he didn't and here we goddamn are.

I know what you're thinking: I was cute as a button and sharp as a knife, so what the fuck happened? I know what I look like. I'm the Elephant Girl now, big bulbous nose and staring eyes and horrible skinny lips all squashed together in the middle of a big moon-face. I stopped looking in mirrors when I was a kid but when I used to go outside there were mirrors everywhere, lurking, waiting for me. Toilets, cafés, shops, even the scruffy stall on the flea market peddling cheap make-up, they all have mirrors winking at each other as my pig-face flashes across them when I go past. And so many fucking windows; in shops, at school, on the buses, in the cars. I'd see myself out of the corner of my eye, see my pasty, fat cheeks and wonky fringe all framed in wood or metal. The mirrors at school were the worst. I hated them. All the girls would be doing their hair and my best mate, Rachel, would be doing her make-up though she knew she'd be told to take it off again by the first teacher who could be arsed to enforce a school rule. She used to cake on foundation, trying to bury her spots though they looked like tiny volcanoes under all that gunk. And she'd paint her lips ruby red and blacken her eyelashes until they were like long spider legs. She wasn't pretty, but she had these big hazel eyes that glowed under all that black. I waited in the toilets by the science block once, until the bell had gone and everyone had run off to class. I wanted to see what I looked like if nobody else was there. And I saw this round-faced fucking halfwit, this horrible thing staring at me and it shocked me so much my mouth opened like I was going to swear but nothing came out. And the thing looked back at me like it was also shocked at what it saw, its mouth just a stupid, round hole in a big fat face. So I punched it. The mirror cracked right across the bottom and some girls came in just as I did it and then ran out to tell the first teacher they saw. My chest started hurting, like it was getting tighter and tighter until I couldn't breathe and I ran out of the school and went home. I punched the mirror over the chest of drawers too, when I first started stopping in here. I thought I'd look different in my own room, dickhead that I am, so I looked. Of course I saw the same thing, my own fucking pig-face. You know what? I like breaking mirrors. I like the sound of the glass smashing and the zigzag pieces hanging onto the frame that can never go back together. Mum took the mirror away, 'to be on the safe side', and a little jagged bit fell off. I've kept it.

I've started cutting my arms again with it. I know they're all manky, I've got eyes, haven't I? It's all that dirt off the floor. Course it fucking hurts. I keep picking at the scabs and it's still all green and runny underneath. It looks like snot but it smells horrible. So do I. Mum says my clothes need washing, but I won't take them off. What's the point? I just sit on the floor anyway and I keep dropping food all over me. I used to try and swipe it all off with my sleeves, but now they're all shiny like my jeans, except my jeans have all these furry streaks on them too. I'm as dirty and greasy as this fucking carpet. I think I can smell myself sometimes when I move, though my nose is clogged with goddamn dust so I don't know how bad it is. Dad always shouted at me when I wet the bed, said I stunk. Mum once heard him and whispered to me, when he'd gone out of the bathroom, not to believe him and I tried to believe her instead. He was always saying that to me when it wasn't true, but now he's not here to say it and I really do stink. That is what my English teacher would call fucking irony. No, I don't think about my dad and no, I don't love my dad. Jesus, you sound like my shrink, all these bloody questions all the bloody time. What? Have you only just seen my fingers? You're not very observant, are you? I bite them, in between popping my hair. Yes, I can see how bad they are, they match my hair. They look disgusting, don't they? Skinny scraps of nail under that big overhang of finger. Of course they fucking hurt! I'm always catching them on my clothes and every time I try to chew them off I take off the skin underneath and then they sting for hours, days sometimes. I'm used to it anyway. Dad used to cut my nails when I was a kid. He'd take the scissors and cut them right down until they hurt like they'd been plunged into boiling water. He'd pull at the corner bits until they popped out and I'd have to suck each finger in turn to stop the bleeding. I could never pick up coins or put my socks on or button my clothes properly for days after. I think that's why I started biting them, so he wouldn't cut them anymore. Stop going on about my nails and my fucking dad. I don't want to talk about that shit. You're always making me talk about stuff I don't want about. I'm going to sleep. You can do one.

．

Hiya, sit yourself down. You can have a biscuit if you like –
but you'll have to run downstairs for it cos I'm a bit restricted
territory-wise, being a fucking hermit. I'm the hostess with
the leastest. I'm the fucking lady of Shallot, me, cursed to
never go outside. Except I hate looking in mirrors. So, nosy
parker, do I love my dad? I used to love him, really love him
when I was little. I can remember when I about 18 months
old, you know. People don't believe me, they say you can't
remember that far back, but I can. I can see loads of times
when I was really small in my mind. It's like it was yesterday.
I was so tiny back then, he was like this big massive giant.
One of my first memories is Dad playing with me. He is
joking around with my brothers and then he comes towards
me and I hide behind Mum, peeping out at him. He hands
me a piece of orange and smiles and I unhook my fingers
from Mum's sleeve and stick my hand out. He pulls it away
and I hesitate, my hand hanging there. He moves it towards
me again and I reach out, hopeful, but he pulls it away again
and makes a funny face, eyes looking at his nose, teeth stuck
out over his top lip. I laugh and laugh to see his funny face
and he gives me the orange. I wasn't scared of him then. Not
even after he beat the living daylights out of me with that
fucking belt of his. I'd go trotting over in my white shoes
whenever I saw him or heard his voice. I'm telling you, I
remember them shoes. And my bonnet that I hated because
it made my ears too hot. And sometimes he'd catch me and
swing me round and it was like I could fit in just one hand, he

was that big. And sometimes he'd shout at me or he'd knock me down and I'd wail but I'd just forget it after a while and run over to him again. I just loved him, again and again and again. I think babies and little kids must only feel one thing at a time. It's either love or hunger or cold or tired. So if something causes pain they feel pain, but when it's gone they go back to their default setting. Babies love the person who feeds them. That was Mum. And they love the people who are the same shape as the people who feed them. That was Dad. And when he hurt me I cried, but the next time I saw him I loved him all over again. Kids are stupid. It was like he kept his temper inside a balloon. He'd go around all happy and smiling and he'd do the gardening or come inside and start wrestling with the lads and me too – if I pestered him long enough – and then we'd sit watching the telly. He even let us kids play out sometimes, when he was like this and we use to dare each other to run in and ask him what was for tea. I usually did it. I loved that feeling of being able to run in and out of the house, like the neighbours' kids could. But every time something annoyed him, the temper balloon got blown up a bit. Like when the chip pan caught fire and he had to run with it through the back door, all the time the flames bending backwards and hitting his face. Even though he was laughing as he poured the hot blaze over the hedge, the balloon inflated a bit. And then something else would happen and the balloon inflated a bit more and a bit more.

We tried, at first, to gauge how full the balloon was.

'Hi-ya, Dad,' we'd say when the back door went. If he said hello back, that was a good sign; it meant jokes and pudding after tea and Mum looking happy for a change. If he only grunted as he came in, that was kind of okay, but it was getting borderline, so we knew that maybe today was okay but tomorrow could be dangerous. And if he said nothing, that was a bad sign. Then our own balloons, *anxiety* balloons, would start inflating. We'd try to keep him in a good mood, asking him did he need anything, and creeping around trying to be noiseless. And if the back door suddenly burst open and his boots clattered over the kitchen tiles we said fuck all. We knew his balloon had been filling all day, away from us, and it was already straining, it couldn't hold any more. And it was these times, when we sat waiting for the bang, waiting and waiting and waiting, pretending that we weren't there as the balloon skin thinned so much we could almost hear the whine of the membrane vibrating. The air itself changed and it got harder to breathe like they say it is up mountains. And there were endless ways to remind him that we existed, to trigger his explosion: pass him the wrong newspaper, trip over his foot, a burp or fart or sneeze that wouldn't stay in, if we shuffled or twitched or tried to scratch an itch or blinked and he caught it in the corner of his eye. If we poked at or whispered to each other or looked far away so that he knew we were thinking thoughts, well, then the balloon went bang. Whoever was in his way would get it. And the rest of us would sit listening to them getting it, the dull whoosh of his boots against skin as if he were kicking a pillow, and him giving a lecture while he did it that he had to work in that shitty job listening to 'Oi, Paddy' a thousand times a day because of us little English bastards, draining his money and his time, his life being wasted in this heathen fuck of a country, that he'd teach us not to talk back to him and that he'd teach us not to look at him like that, not to go laughing and whispering behind his fucking back. A family of fucking balloons.

There were a load of other things that I knew made him angry: that we could all read and write better than him because his mother never let him go to school. He ripped up my book when I was ten, because I was laughing at something in it, and Mum had to pay because it was from the library. He hated that we knew more about where things were in the world, that we knew how rivers were formed and what coal was made of and where aardvarks came from, that I was a girl but I knew words he'd never even heard of, that

I could run away inside a book but he couldn't get past the entrance. We moved around him like crabs, sideways on so we could always see him. We spoke like ghosts might speak, in whispers and murmurs, so that the noise didn't carry. But still he swelled and swelled with anger. When the balloon had burst, he'd grab one of us and start battering and when it was over he'd march into the garden or shed and do stuff that made a lot of noise and we'd all slip silently upstairs to see whoever Mum had put to bed. When Dad came back to the house he'd be quiet, like his batteries had gone, and there'd be a space where we could kind of move normally again. And then he'd become over-playful with Tommo and Jamie, tickling them until they were nearly sick or doing his 'bay-ting' game. I used to stand by the sofa where he play-fought them and they'd do this funny thing with their eyes rolling white when his arms reached a hold of them. We would be noisy then as well; we would laugh and even scream sometimes. Dad hardly ever wrestled with me but I could make noises on the sidelines. I always had a backlog of noise to get through, a mass of sounds to get out. I used to squeak and squeal and make a sound like an air-raid siren and the lads would roar like mini-dads. We bounced between happy dad and angry dad like fucking tennis balls, until we didn't know anymore which one we were about to collide with and I did my loyal little dog thing for about ten fucking years. When my brothers got angry after one of us had been leathered, they'd say really bad things about him and until I was older, I'd get really angry with them and run into my room and sit by myself. And I'd try to go back to their room later but they wouldn't let me in so I'd sit outside, squawking and saying through the door, 'I love my daddy.' When the NSPCC first came to see us, when I was about six, they asked me the same bloody question. A lady knelt by me, rolling my sleeves up and my socks down, pulling up my jumper so that all my bruises were on show. Two men did the same to my brothers.

'Do you love your daddy, Amanda?' the lady said.

I looked at Dad, stood in the corner, watching me. 'Yes,' I said. 'But I don't think Daddy loves me.'

The lady took a hanky out of her sleeve and flapped it until it opened into a big square and she put her face in it for ages and when she took her face out it was all wet.

I love my daddy. Jesus Christ. Like Dad always said, I was a stupid little bastard.

You're like a fucking bad penny. I thought you were Mr K for a minute. I've haven't seen him in ages. I wouldn't speak to him last time. He gave me a cassette tape just before I stopped going to school again. He said it was full of singers I'd like. And then he said, 'They know how it feels, you know, to be you.' The music was great, so I doubt they have a fucking clue what it's like to be me. He'd even put in a list of who they all were, Joan Baez, Joni Mitchell, Janis Joplin, who I love because she screamed when she sang and I felt like it was me singing. One side was full of Bob Dylan songs and I loved it. It was better that anything I'd heard in the charts, all the crap by Iron Maiden that my brothers were into, or Duran Duran and Spandau Ballet who the girls at school were slobbering over. There were proper words, little stories being told. I played my tape once to my cousin over the road but she just laughed and said he hadn't got a note in his head. I don't care what she thinks, she's backward. She tried to get in here once, about six months back. I heard her talking to Mum and I was thinking, For fuck's sake, don't let *her* up here. She came to the door and was knocking for ages and then she just pushed it open, trying to look through the fucking door. I slammed it in her face and she ran down the stairs, saying, 'Everyone says you're mental.' I heard Mum shouting at her and then the front door banged. I screamed for about a fucking hour and banged my head against the door until Mum said she was going to have to get the ambulance. I've not done any of that headbanging since then. I can't be arsed. I don't want to talk to anyone anymore. Mr K kept asking why I wouldn't answer him and he sounded sad and so I put my fingers in my ears until he went away. I'm not going to cry anymore. I don't need to. I pull at my hair, pop, pop, pop! I don't give a shit. I feel the same way inside that my legs do when I've sat on them too long or my mouth does after the dentist, all rubbery and far away, like I don't belong to me.

Part Four
Battered

Amanda doesn't go to school on Friday mornings anymore because she goes to see the psychologist. She has learned to say the word but she can't remember what it means. When she asked Aunty Pammy why she was going there, she told her it was to 'see a hospital man so he can see what a clever girl you are', but Amanda doesn't believe her because her mum is always cross when they go for the bus. They are walking up the very steep hill to the hospital. Amanda is trailing slightly, the fingers on her free hand bouncing off the railings. Her other hand is red-hot despite the wind slamming into her as she climbs; the heat from it has gone through her glove and is finally making her mum's cold hand slightly warm. Amanda has been coming here since she stopped learning at school, sat instead, hearing nothing, feeling like she was sliding around inside her own tummy, until she thought she might be asleep and dreaming. She likes coming here now, likes playing the games and being asked all the questions. On the first visit, Amanda stuck close to her mum and even when she spotted the huge box of toys, she didn't move, just kept looking at the jumble of bricks and cars and books and dolls. In the end she dragged her mum with her when she went to investigate them. The hospital man had thick glasses that were dirty and his eyes were as tiny as Mole in her *Wind in the Willows* book. He bent down to the toy box and asked Amanda how old she was.

'Tell him you're seven in two months,' her mum said.

Amanda got up and ran to her mum, whispering in her ear, 'He's got worms in his beard.'

'Don't be silly,' her mum said, and got hold of her shoulders and turned her around to see him. The worms turned out to be his mouth, fat, wet pink lips in the midst of a curly tangle of beard. When he closed them together, they made a squiggle so his mouth looked as if it were squirming. He's got a face full of animals, Amanda thought. Her mum squashes a tissue up to her nose and tells her to blow.

'How are you Amanda? My name is Dr Charles. I'm going to chat with your mum for a while, in that room there. You can play with any toy you like.' He smiles as he speaks but Amanda stops what she is doing, dropping the toy cow she'd been playing with, tears filling her eyes. She watches the man close the door to his room and she wants to run to them. He stands at the window of his room, watching her. Her mum is next to him and she sees their mouths moving, first his, then her mums. His mouth moves a lot more than her mums. Amanda feels glued to the floor but when her mum comes out and calls her, she springs to her feet and comes running, her feet sliding on the purple nylon carpet. The man puts out a third chair for Amanda and then moves behind his desk and sits opposite her mum. The brown plastic feels greasy under her fingers so she slides off and stands next to her mum, who shuffles in her seat, away from her, so she moves closer again and if feels like they are doing a kind of dance, swaying away and together, away and together, before her mum tuts and lets Amanda get as close as she wants.

The man takes off his glasses and rubs the lenses against his sleeve. He gets a wooden jigsaw picture of a horse and pushes it towards Amanda and then mixes it up on the table. Amanda loves horses; she used to talk to the horse in the field on the way to school until one day it was no longer there.

'Can you put this back together?' the man asks.

Amanda reaches out and places the biggest shape back in the wooden frame and straightens it. She then takes each piece in turn, holding the peg sticking out of it and twisting it in her fingers and then matching it to the shapes already put back. When she gets to the last piece, a single long slice of brown, she tries to push it into the waiting space where it doesn't quite fit, its edge just outside the neat line of the other pieces. The man reaches for it and Amanda jumps backwards and puts her face against her mum's chest.

'Ow. For God's sake, be careful, Amanda May.' Her mum pushes her back and she can feel the edge of the man's desk jabbing her in the back.

'Don't be scared, Amanda,' the man says. 'You're doing really well.'

She watches him wiggle the pieces to increase the gap and then turns the last piece upside down so that it becomes part of the horse's neck. He smiles and hands Amanda a book with a boy and a girl on swings on the front.

'Please can you read for me? I hear you're very good.'

Amanda flicks from one page to the next until she sees a picture of the girl sat at a table blowing out birthday candles. She has bright red shoes with shiny buckles and white ribbons in her hair. Amanda puts her fingers on the pink cake.

'Read it then, love,' her mum says.

Words tumble out of Amanda, so fast she barely stops one word before she starts the next one.

'Wow! That's great. You're very clever.'

'It's a little kid's book. It's too easy-peasy.'

'Ah! Do you not like this book?'

'Yes, I do. I want to live inside it.'

He laughs.

'It would be a nice place to live, that's for sure. This is the last one for today, Amanda,' he says, and places a large sheet with long words in thick black ink in front of her.

'They look like boats, sailing,' Amanda says. 'On a big white sea.'

'They do, indeed. Can you read this word for me?' and he points at the first word.

Amanda keeps reading word after word, even as the letters multiply. After a dozen or so she stops, her lips moving again as she tries the latest word to herself.

'Pie-see-col-og-gee,' she said.

'Wow! Almost right. Psychology. That's very, very good. How do you feel reading such a big word?'

'Dizzy,' Amanda says, and he laughs again and her mum laughs too. And Amanda laughs along with them. She wants to keep laughing but her mum shushes her and says to be quiet now.

The man stands up.

'We've finished for today. It's been very nice to meet you, Amanda. I'll see you again next week, okay?'

He walks to the door with them and smiles and waves and Amanda lifts her hand and waves back. She keeps looking back and waving until he goes back inside. Then she turns around and gets free of her mum's hand and skips, chattering, down to the gate that leads to the hill.

By the time her mum drops her off at school it is break time. The wind blows around her legs and up the sleeves of her coat as she walks across the playground and stands by the toilet wall near to where her teacher, Mrs Ogden, is talking to the caretaker. Amanda watches the children playing as she fishes in her coat pocket for a hanky, watches them running and skipping and some of them walking around in pairs. She is shuffling her feet to keep warm as the four girls from her class walk up to her, the way they do every day. Susan glares at her and points to her nose.

'Your snot isn't like ours. It's all green.'

Amanda sniffs loudly and sticks a finger up her nostril to try and push it back inside. The girls laugh.

'Green snot. Green snot,' Susan chants, and the others join in.

She stands perfectly still and says nothing, trying not to sniff. Susan starts running and the others follow her. They

chant, green snot, as they run away. Mrs Ogden turns round
to look at her, then she turns back, still talking. A swelling,
like a hiccup, fills her insides, begins to hurt as if she needs to
burp. She hears a voice, strangely soft, calling to her.

'Amanda – hey, Manda.'

When the voice keeps going, she looks around but there is
nobody near her. The voice returns, deeper and louder.

'Amanda, I've got something for you.'

She sees her dad on the road at the bottom edge of the
schoolyard. He is holding out a pear to her through the iron
railings.

'Come here,' he says. His eyes are two red circles with his
eyes shining like torches in the middle, and when he speaks,
his mouth becomes another red circle in his face. Eventually
she moves forward and reaches for the pear. The wind catches
her skirt and her thighs, a mass of thick purple and black
bruises, show for a minute before her skirt flops back down.
She snatches the pear from his hand.

'Go on, eat it,' her dad says.

The pear is yellow on one side and red on the other, like
Snow White's apple. When the bell rings her dad waves
and walks away, and she puts the pear on the wall under the
climbing frame. She has to run to get to the line in time. She
gets her maths book and her pencil ready, as she does every
week, rolling it between her finger and thumb. Mrs Ogden
reads out times tables questions and Amanda thinks of the
man at the hospital and all the games he has and she can
hear the teacher today. The answers fly into her brain and she
writes them all down, in neat little rows in her book. When
the home bell rings, she runs outside and the pear is gone,
and she doesn't know if it had ever existed, if maybe Dad
hadn't been there at all.

Her mum is waiting after school but they don't walk home.
Instead they wait at the school gate until her brothers come
up the road swinging their bags in circles. A sad-looking

man says hello to them and then her mum tells her to get in his car.

'Where are we going?' she asks her.

'To see a friend of your brothers,' she says.

'Oh, he'll be glad to see you all,' the man says, 'he enjoys having visitors.'

Amanda doesn't know who he means. Her mum sits in the front and talks a little bit to the man but he doesn't answer so then it goes quiet. When they get to the house, it is in the middle of a row of tiny, slanted houses. Amanda files into the living room behind the man, her brothers and her mum. A woman rushes up to them, all flapping arms and red eyes and jittery hands. She drags the boys to seats opposite a bed.

'Look, Andrew; James and Thomas are here to see you,' she says.

The boy waves weakly at them.

'Hello,' Tommo and Jamie say at the same time.

The woman takes Amanda's hand and they go into the kitchen where Jammie Dodgers are dished up onto a plate and handed to her. When she goes back into the front room, she is given a seat next to Tommo. It is a little bit too high and she sits with her tiptoes touching the floor and the biscuits sliding towards the edge of the plate.

When she finally looks at the bed, she sees a skeleton-boy with huge eyes and bare arms, thin as twigs. His skin stretches over jutting bones and his body, half the size of her, looks all crumpled up under the bright red blanket that covers him. His lips are curled away from his teeth that look huge in his tiny monkey face. The room is really hot with the fire on full. It smells like the nurse's office at school. Amanda tilts the plate upwards just in time to stop the biscuits dropping onto the floor.

'Is he like this because of the cancer?' Tommo says to the woman.

'For God's sake,' Amanda's mum says, who is sat on a short stool gripping her handbag. She hasn't stopped smiling since she got there and her mouth is a long, bright red line in her face.

'It's okay,' Andrew's mother says. 'He was doing really well, love, but then he caught pneumonia, he's been this poorly ever since.'

Amanda wants to take off her coat but she daren't ask anyone. She is afraid of the skeleton-boy, whose skin is yellow and who is now looking at her. He doesn't move, at all, or speak. Maybe, she thinks, it's because he didn't wash his hands after going to the loo. Her mum got very angry when Jamie didn't wash his hands, said he could get sick with germs.

'He's very happy to see you,' the woman says.

Amanda doesn't think he looks happy.

'Does anyone want a drink?' she asks.

'No, thank you,' Amanda's mum says.

Amanda and her brothers shake their head. The woman is looking at Amanda's brothers, who look at their knees. She looks from one to the other and then at Amanda's mum who is still smiling, hard, as if something is wedged inside her mouth.

'Well, he's getting tired now,' the woman says.

Amanda's mum jumps to her feet and Amanda and her brothers do the same.

'Shall I run you back?' the man says.

'No, we'll be fine on the bus,' Amanda's mum tells him.

They leave the room, one by one through the narrow door. On the way home, Amanda's mum stops, twice, to get a tissue from her bag, wipes her eyes and puts it back again.

They get on the bus and are allowed to sit upstairs. Amanda tells herself she must remember to wash her hands when she gets home in case the germs have got into her body. If she forgets she will get sick. The germs will twist her up until she also looks like a pile of bent sticks.

The warmth of the piss, after trying to hold it in for hours, instead of getting up for the toilet and risk waking her dad, gives a strange kind of comfort, but that quickly gives over to cold wetness that sets all the hairs on her legs shivering as the sodden part of the sheet tickles at them. She curls her body away from the centre of the bed, which is soaked, so that her back is right up against the cold of the wall. She feels like a caterpillar balancing on top of a twig. One leg cramps so she lifts it and places it on top of the other leg, right foot on left ankle. The cramp eases but the ankle bone starts to ache so she turns over, crouches into a foetal position on the opposite side of the bed, as far away from the piss as she can get without falling out of bed. Her legs keep slipping back into the cold and wet but she tries to sleep, waiting for what is coming in the morning.

Mum used to get her up but she never sees her in the morning any more. She is still in bed when everyone else leaves the house. Instead, Dad bursts into the bedroom.

'You'd better not have done it again.'

Amanda doesn't say anything, which tells him that that she has.

'Get up out of that bed, you dirty little pig.'

She's not quick enough to scoot across the damp bit of mattress so he drags her over the side of the bed and drops her on the floor with a dull thump.

'Get here, now.'

By the time she's picked herself up and gone after him, he is standing in the bathroom doorway. She runs past him as quickly as she can but he shoves her and she stumbles, knocking her knees against the burgundy plastic bath panel that squeals and bends a little. It doesn't really hurt. He often makes her wash in cold water, but today Mum came in and turned both taps on and she can see the steam rising. She takes off her nightie and gets into the bath. The water is warm against the cold morning air that creeps through the window. Just as Dad picks up the soap, someone shouts loudly just outside the house. Bonnie has been waiting in the hedge for

84

the milkman again. He's yelling at the dog, which is making her so excited she starts making her high yak-yak noises. Amanda can see her in her mind, taking off vertically like the army planes she saw in her brothers' comics, jumping chest high to the milkman to show him how much she likes his game of shouting.

'Fucking English idiot,' Dad says, and throws the soap at the bath as he goes to see to the dog. It smacks into the water and splashes water into her eyes. With her dad gone, she washes herself as quickly as she can. She looks at the bubble bath Aunty Pammy got her for her birthday, sitting in the little dent by the hot tap. The bottle is shaped like a fish standing on its tail and it makes the water green, but she daren't use it. Instead, she pushes herself up to the end of the bath and slides back down which forces the water up over her, then moves her legs in the water to make waves. The warm water chops up over her tummy. She hears Dad joking with the milkman who is laughing a lot, which is good because he won't report the dog. Dad can make anyone laugh, at the exact time he wants them to. Amanda knows this because she was in the shop with her mum once and the neighbour Mrs Eaton said, 'That husband of yours can certainly turn on the Irish charm.' Mum didn't say anything back and just stood looking at her until Mrs Eaton got all red and pretended to search through her purse for something.

As they were walking home, Amanda asked her what she'd meant and Mum had told her about Dad getting everyone to laugh when he wants them to. Her mum said it as if she was very angry. Mum hardly answers anyone anymore. And she's stopped singing when she does the washing up. Amanda sits up and eases the tap on, quietly and slowly. The new, hotter water bubbles under the water already in the bath and grabs at her legs. She pretends that she is a mermaid in the sea with hair made of seaweed. The deep sea is cold to humans, but to the mermaid it is warm as soup. Hot waves heat her body as she swims and looks out for fish and other mermaids to chase.

She holds her head under the surface of the sea, listening to the water rushing over the rocks, loud as a waterfall.

Dad bursts in to the bathroom.

'Switch that fucking tap off, now.'

She slips and slides in the bath and eventually manages to sit upright. She didn't hear him coming up the stairs in her mermaid world.

He grabs her hair, no longer made of seaweed, and shakes her head back, slaps her face, bangs her head on the wall.

'I'm sorry, I'm sorry,' she says, but he isn't listening.

'Wasting water, you little bastard,' he shouts.

He takes the saucepan they use for rinsing our hair, fills it with cold water and throws it over her.

'Get out of that fucking bath,' he says, blocking the door.

She pulls herself out of the bath and stands by the sink, as far from him as possible in the tiny room, knowing that she is too late to dry herself. Now he will do it. He is rough on her skin, it hurts, especially her armpits and stomach and *down there*. She keeps her eyes on her feet. He stops abruptly.

'Jesus, I hate you,' he shouts, throwing the towel into the bath. 'And all those kids at school hate you too, because you *stink*.'

He stands in the doorway again. She runs past him into the bedroom, arms up, crossed above her head but he doesn't strike her. Her brothers come into the bedroom just after she has got dressed. They have their angry faces on, the ones they use when Dad can't see them. Amanda looks for her jumper, finds it in the folds of the damp bed.

'Nobody hates...' Tommo says, but Amanda pushes at him until he shuts up and they all leave the bedroom together.

They go downstairs and sit silently at the table. Three bowls are laid out, cereal and milk inside. Dad always pours too much sugar on the cornflakes so Amanda tries to swallow without tasting it. They bolt their food as quickly as they can then grab their bags and coats and run outside.

They used to walk to school together but now her brothers get the bus to their junior school so Amanda has to take a right through the graveyard by herself. Her church is next to the primary school. She doesn't know what kind this is, except that it's non-Catholic. As soon as she is on her own she dawdles along the gravel path that cuts directly through the middle of the graves and then she gets a funny feeling, like her legs don't want her to go forward any more. Her legs turn and walk her down to the fields bordering the church where they sit her bottom down on her school bag. She looks at the sky to see if it's going to rain but the clouds look lazy, like they just want to hang around with her, not really doing anything. She sniffs at her jumper to see if she can smell anything but she can't decide if she can or not. She pokes a twig at the ground and she watches the cows drifting, wondering what they might say to each other. After a while, she stands up, picks up her bag and sets off through the dry grass, meandering, without direction, into the day.

She is lying, hungry and chilled, on the top of the hill just opposite the house. The hill, like Amanda, is solitary, standing separate from the bigger, rolling hills that lead to the reservoir where they swim in the summer, a tiny island in the moorland sea. There is a police car outside the house, shining white in the fading light like a fallen star at the edge of the garden. A lot of the neighbours are out in their gardens. Amanda can hear her mum and Aunty Pammy calling for her, circling the field nearest the house as they shout. Her dad has already gone up the street. She watched him heading towards the old tip at the back of the factory where they found her last time, wandering through the broken bottles and crates and cardboard.

Amanda wants to go home. Strange shadows dance together, creeping up the sides of the hill or leaping up at the blackened clouds. Things crouch with her in the dark, stroking the back of her neck and making soft thumping noises all around her. She screams, an astonishing noise that explodes into the silence to send the night things rattling away and then hangs in the sky like a flare. The scream unpins Amanda's frozen limbs like a magic spell and she scrabbles down the lumpy ground through high grown weeds that knot around her ankles like snares. She falls, running full pelt onto sharp stones and rolls the rest of the way down. As she picks herself up she hears her aunty Pammy, close by, shouting.

'I'm coming, I'm coming. It's okay, love. I'm coming.'

They collide at the bottom of the white path, elbows clashing as they grope for each other in the dimness. She folds Amanda into her, tucks her inside one arm as the other circles her shoulders and she tugs gently at her hair with her fingers. Amanda burrows into the warmth of her, into the safety of her solid body.

'Why do you have to do this? What were...? Oh, Jesus and Mary, he's going to bloody kill you now.'

She takes Amanda's hand. As they walk through the gloom Amanda feels their footsteps, two steps for every one of her aunty's. Aunty Pammy opens the gate just as Seamus appears, a policeman at his side like a bodyguard. Amanda is hit with a barrage of words. First the policeman, then her dad, then her dad and the policeman together, then the policeman at her dad, saying something about giving him room to speak. She nods and nods through all this angry droning until her neck hurts. The policeman leaves and they go inside the house and stand in the front room where Seamus says he's going to get his cane.

'She's had too much today. Leave it now,' her aunty Pammy says, and she takes his hand off the door handle and pushes it shut. When he doesn't open it again, she sits down on the sofa and pulls Amanda down beside her. Seamus shouts and shouts, leaning towards her at one point and wagging his finger in her face. And through it all, Aunty

Pammy's hand is fastened tightly around Amanda's until her palm pulsates – thump, thump, thump – like a shared secret that Dad doesn't know.

She is not afraid of the man at the hospital now, or his beard. Amanda has a heap of questions when her mum comes to collect her from school. She asks what she might be doing today, will she be drawing or will it be all words or will he let her play with his tape recorder again? And she says how she has thought of lots of things to tell him, about how the bus bounces and rattles and shakes. When they get there, she no longer clings to her mum's side but runs up to greet him and takes his hand as she goes into his room. He has a present for her this week. It is a bag of coloured pencils. There are ten, she counted them, and they shimmer in the packet when she holds it to the light. He gives her a badge too, that says *I'm the best*.

'We can finish today Amanda. I'm very pleased with you, joining in at school again.' He starts to talk to her mother, smiling away. Amanda starts to cry.

'But I've not done my puzzles,' she says.

'You don't have to do any tests today,' the hospital man says.

'I want to.'

'It's time to go,' her mum says.

'I'm not going until I've done my puzzles.'

The hospital man hunkers down beside her.

'Amanda, I'm sorry that we have to end today,' he says. 'I want you to know that I'm very proud of you.'

Amanda yells at him.

'I'm not bloody going.'

Her mother gives her a slap across the bottom and marches her out of his room. She runs to the toy box and clings on to the edge. Her mum peels Amanda's fingers off roughly and drags her by the arm to get her moving. Her shoulder hurts where her mum yanked it and when she gets to the gate she realises that the pencils are still on the hospital man's desk. She takes the badge out of her pocket and digs the pin again and again into her cheek, and then holds it there until blood trickles, warm and wet and thick against her hand.

She laughs when the sausage her dad is holding on his fork drops and falls with a splat into the middle of his mash, spraying the front of his shirt with tiny freckles of brown sauce. The first punch hits her in the arm and it goes hot as if it is scalded. She ducks under the next one and runs away and he is after her, knocking over his chair in his hurry to grab her. He catches one ankle and drags her backwards but Amanda kicks herself loose and scrabbles up the stairs to the tiny square landing where the stairs turn ninety degrees. She sits there watching him.

'Get down here,' he says softly.

She tries to stand but her legs don't work. Only her hands move, flapping around her like two baby birds learning how to fly.

'If I have to come up there to get you, by Jesus I'll make it worse for yer. Move yer fucking self.'

Rapid, tiny stings zigzag when she breathes, like a splinter is lodged inside her. She pulls herself up by putting one arm on the wall and one on the banister, but when she lets go her legs buckle and she slides on her bum back down the seven steps to land at Seamus' feet. He grabs her by her hair, a generous handful in each hand, and tries to pull her to her feet but she is heavy in his hands and slumps so he throws her against the staircase.

She cries out as her knee twists when she lands.

'Dad, please.'

She hears Tommo, somewhere behind the bulk of her dad.

'Fuck off outside, now.'

She hears them run to the door, hears the soft bang as it hits the wall and she curls up, tight as a spring bud and waits.

Mum has burnt the fish fingers again. Amanda pushes them around her plate until she feels her dad's eyes on her and she quickly lifts a forkful and chews. Her dad gets up and scrapes his food into the bin. Her mum says nothing, keeps eating. It's raining so after they eat, Amanda and Tommo file into the front room where Dad is watching the news. Jamie comes in with Dad's mug, full to the brim, tea rippling. Just as he gets to their dad's chair he loses his balance and the hot tea splashes everywhere, on their dad's trousers, over the chair arm, some arcs backwards and sprays her and Tommo. Jamie stands still as a statue. Their dad slaps the back of his head, propelling it down and he almost falls, spindly arms frantically trying to steady the cup. Their mum jumps up from the sofa just as their dad brings his clenched fist down on the top of Jamie's head.

'Yer stupid little bastard.'

'Seamus, for Christ's sake.' Mum puts herself in front of Jamie, blocking Dad's way. Amanda grabs hold of her mum's skirt and Tommo grabs Jamie, pulling him clear of Dad's arm span.

'Fucking move.'

'Stop it. Jesus, stop it!' she screams. 'Not again. Not this shit again.'

Barbara herds them into the kitchen and peels off Jamie's wet T-shirt. They all stared at the bright pink specks where the hot drink has hit him, like tiny bits of bubble gum, splattered across his ribs.

They are all in her brother's bedroom, Amanda, Tommo, Jamie, their mum, huddled together on the bottom bunk. Their arms and thighs, sticking out of T-shirt sleeves and shorts, are so mottled with bruises they look cold, but the Penguin biscuits their mum has snuck upstairs to them are melting in the heat of their hands. It has gone quiet downstairs.

Aunty Pammy still comes round but whenever her dad comes in, Aunty Pammy disappears, like the figures in cuckoo clocks. Granny and Grandad have stopped coming round and they're not allowed to go visit them because of the fight they had with Dad. She heard her gran and granddad and Aunty Pammy in the front room so she peeped round the door. Her grandad was stood up next to her dad and her gran and Aunty Pammy sat with her mum on the couch, their arms around her as she cried.

'Nippers need a belt here and there but you're going much too far,' her grandad says.

'Keep that big nose of yours out,' her dad says.

'Don't you dare talk to my father like that,' her mum says.

'That'd be right. Must behave for the holy fucking trinity,' her dad says.

'That's enough of that, lad,' her grandad says.

Words fire from one side of the room to the other. It's the first time she's heard her mum shout directly at her dad and she moves to try and see her mum more clearly. She sees her dad move right up close to her grandad and her grandad looks at her dad, shorter, frailer, but unafraid.

'What's going on, Mum?' she says, and heads turn. Her gran cranes her neck round and shushes everyone, and her dad pushes past her grandad and then her and stomps across the kitchen and out the door. After a while he appears framed in the window like he's on the TV, chopping at the long grass where the garden backs onto the jungle at the side.

'Go out and play,' her mum says. She doesn't want to leave in case something changes while she is not there and she hesitates for a while. Her mum begins to say something, the few words tumble fast and angry. Her aunty Pammy gets up and wraps an arm around her shoulders, where it lies warm and tingly on her skin, and takes her into the hall. She helps her into a coat and ties her trainers for her, puts ten pence into her hand and then opens the door, kisses her nose and waves her off.

Her grandad is at the school every day, he's the lollipop man, but he doesn't walk her home anymore. He waits with her until her mum arrives, asking her about what she's learned, speaks to her mum for a few minutes and then heads off in the opposite direction.

Amanda heard him say one time, 'I'm worried about them kids.'

'Me too,' her mum says.

Amanda watches her grandad getting smaller as he heads towards the road and when she turns round, her mum has already started walking. Amanda has to run fast to catch up to her.

'Which one of you little fucking animals didn't flush the toilet?' her dad says, his walking stick in hand. None of them answer.

'Line up,' he says.

They don't move a muscle. 'I won't tell you again,' he says. They get up slowly and stand in a row in front of him.

'Put your hands out.'

'Dad, no,' Jamie says but he puts his hand out anyway. Amanda and Tommo do the same, hands stretched away from their bodies, palms facing up. They bob up and down like kites caught in a breeze. Their dad swings the stick down hard on each hand in turn. Jamie gasps, his mouth opening and closing like a caught fish. Amanda tries not to look at him as his face, already too thin and white, gets even paler. She can't bear it when he looks like his own ghost. Before her dad has time to raise the stick again she clenches her fists against her thighs, and says, 'It was me.'

'Sit down,' Dad tells her brothers and their bodies jolt, arms flailing, legs tangling against each other as they scramble for the sofa.

'Please, Dad, I'm sorry, I'm sorry,' Amanda says, shuffling backwards. 'Please, I'm sorry.'

He moves closer and one of Amanda's legs flinches sideways. She pulls it back in quickly just as her dad swings the cane to and fro, across her shoulders and down her back to her thighs. He throws the stick over the top of the boys' heads and it bounces off the sofa cushion and then lands, circus-trick style, perfectly upright by the fireplace.

'Move yerself, yer dirty little faggot,' he says, and stamps out of the room. Laurel and Hardy are on the TV. Hardy thumps Laurel who falls onto his bottom. Amanda and Laurel exchange glances. Laurel begins to cry, rubbing his hair with his fingers. Amanda doesn't cry, not anymore.

Amanda is picked up from school by her aunty Pammy who gives her a new satchel for her birthday and then lets her run around in the field on the way home. She runs into the kitchen and takes a handful of crushed bluebells out of the bag and tries to give them to her mum who is putting burgers under the grill. Her mum points a finger at the table. She puts them down by the plate of bread and butter. Jamie and Tommo run in. Tommo's face is badly cut across the cheek.

'What on earth have you been doing now?' Aunty Pammy says.

'It wasn't our fault, they started it,' Jamie and Tommo say, almost together. Tommo stumbles as he tries to get to the kitchen bench.

'Help me, Mum,' Tommo says. 'Help me.'

'It's okay, love,' Aunty Pammy says, 'I'm right here.'

Amanda stands with her mother at the door, watching the ambulance park by the house across the road. Mr Williams walks his son, who sports a bloody bandage on his head, into the vehicle, talking all the while with his wife, who gestures at the Duffys' house and then marches up the road, in the direction of the factory, in her slippers.

'Christ, Pamela, it's Angela's lad. She'll not let this go. Jamie, go into the garden and see which way she goes.'

Amanda tries to cuddle up to Tommo but he is as stiff as the sheets Mum left on the line last winter.

Ten minutes later, Jamie runs back in the house. 'Mum, Dad's coming. He's running down the road.'

Tommo starts to rock back and forth in the chair. His arms are wrapped around his chest, spluttering words as he moves.

'Tommo,' Aunty Pammy says. 'Listen to me. Get up and run to Gran's. Now.' Tommo doesn't move so Amanda shoves him, over and over.

'Go to Gran's. Go on Tommo. Get to Gran's,' she says.

When Seamus throws the front door open, he makes a beeline for Tommo.

'You're not touching him,' Aunty Pammy says, and tries to push Seamus back. He hits her across the face and sends her flying into the wall as he grabs Tommo and carries him out of the room. Amanda hears Tommo pleading as he is dragged up the stairs, begging forgiveness, saying he'll never do it again. Barbara helps Aunty Pammy up and they both fly up the stairs, heels rapping like hooves.

'Seamus, leave him alone, for fuck's sake.'

It is the first time Amanda has heard Aunty Pammy say that word and she looks at Jamie who is rolled into a ball like a hedgehog, his face hidden underneath his arms. She runs up the stairs and sees her aunty Pammy wedged in the doorway of the bedroom. Seamus slams the door against her, again and again, until she cries out and has to turn her soft body away from its hard edge. Then she is outside and the door is shut and heavy furniture scrapes across the floor then thumps against the door. Tommo screams and the note is long and loud and high. Then they hear Seamus get to work. Muffled thumps come through the door.

Aunty Pammy and her mum are hammering on the door.

'Seamus, stop it. For fuck's sake, come out.'

Amanda's mum turns round.

'Get help,' she says, 'now.'

Amanda runs outside and sees the neighbours' gardens all empty, except for the house opposite where Mrs Broadbent is planting flowers. She runs to her as Tommo's screams explode out of the house. Mrs Broadbent backs away from Amanda, her trowel held in front of her like a gun, until she reaches her back door. She goes into her house backwards. Amanda stands in the street thinking that she will come back out with her husband, but then she sees their curtains being drawn. She hears Tommo scream one last time, cut short by a loud thud and Amanda turns around and stares up at her brothers' bedroom window as her dad's figure moves in and out of view.

'I'm sorry,' she whispers, 'I'm sorry.'

When she wakes up, she is no longer in the street but in bed, and she jumps up, ready to prove to herself that it hasn't happened. When she opens the bedroom door, she hears voices downstairs so she goes down, jumping three and four stairs at a time. She bursts into the kitchen and runs straight into her aunty Pammy who is heaving two big suitcases across the floor.

'I was just coming to find you. There is no school today. We're going on a holiday. Hurry up and get ready,' Aunty Pammy says.

'Where's Mum?'

'She's upstairs, helping Tommo get dressed.'

'Where's Dad?'

'Shake a leg, that's a good girl. We've not got long before the taxi comes.'

She goes back upstairs and Jamie comes out of his room already dressed but not in his uniform. He has red eyes and he is carrying a plastic bag stuffed full of his comics. Amanda runs into her room and puts on her best top, the pink one with the buttons in the shape of flowers. She can't find her jeans so she puts on her checked trousers and trainers. Aunty Pammy comes in and picks up her teddy, now dirty-white and half bald, a thread of ribbon hanging from its neck.

'I'm too old for that,' Amanda tells her.

'You might want it sometime.'

Amanda doesn't see how she'll need it on holiday but she likes Aunty Pammy helping her so she says nothing else as a few books and her notepaper and pens are thrown into the suitcase along with a heap of clothes pulled out of drawers. Sleeves and socks now dangle untidily from the open drawers but her aunty Pammy doesn't put them away, just clicks the catches on the case.

As they walk out of the bedroom, Aunty Pammy calls behind her, 'Barbara, I can hear the taxi.'

Amanda stands with Jamie in the hall. She gets hold of his hand and instead of shrugging her off he wraps both his hands around hers. Aunty Pammy comes down with the second case and then she runs back up. When Tommo appears, hanging between Aunty Pammy and her mum, his ashen face is sticking out from some kind of dark scarf. His legs don't work properly and she can see sweat streaming from her mum and her aunty as they carry him down. He looks like he is sleepwalking. His eyes flicker open then close. When they reach the bottom step Amanda sees that that he isn't wearing a scarf at all. The skin on his neck and up around his ears is black with bruises.

'Open the door, love,' Aunty Pammy says.

Jamie tugs open the door and lets them through. And they struggle, all of them, to the taxi. Amanda and Jamie struggle with a case apiece, her aunty and mum with the dead weight of Tommo, who struggles to move at all. In the taxi, Aunty Pammy starts crying, tears running down her face and then her mum joins in. Amanda knows that people don't cry if they're going on holiday and thinks maybe they're going to the hospital to fix up Tommo, except they've got all these cases and she's got her teddy and it doesn't make any sense. She is frightened at all the crying and she joins in and then Jamie starts too. The only one not crying is Tommo. He is slumped against Aunty Pammy, eyes rolling in his sockets, making a humming noise, like a fridge.

'Did Dad come for the dog?' Barbara says. Aunty Pammy nods.

'Where are we going?' Amanda says. 'Where are we going?' When nobody answers her, she starts pulling at her hair with both hands until her mum hugs her. The touch of her mum is so unfamiliar and so unexpected, that it makes her feel funny, as if Bonnie had suddenly talked.

They are greeted by a skinny woman with baggy trousers that puff out around her. She doesn't smile and has deep lines around her mouth. She ushers them inside and takes them immediately up the wide stone staircase. She stands in front of a locked door and turns the key in a padlock.

The door groans as it opens onto a huge room with two beds in it.

'You'll have to share beds, we're full up. And there is a problem with mice, but don't worry about it. The council are coming to sort it. Settle them in and come down to the office.' She pushes the key into Barbara's hands and then she is gone.

The only wall with a window in it is splattered across its wide lower half with huge shit-coloured stains. The window is long and wide and Amanda looks out at the wall that surrounds the house. The gate looks as big and thick as a castle drawbridge. A huge wooden cabinet teeters unsteadily in one corner and there's a white plasticky-looking set of drawers that has burn marks on the top.

Her mother helps Tommo onto one of the beds.

'Help me with the cases, Barbara,' Aunty Pammy says, 'you two, go and look around until we've finished.'

Amanda and Jamie stick tight to each other as they inch down the corridor and then down the stairs. It is a noisy place. They can hear doors slamming, feet running up and down, low voices that sound like people are trapped inside the walls. The disembodied voices float along with them and then sink under the high-pitched yelling of children. At the bottom of the stairs they don't know which way to go. Suddenly a woman's bony face pops out of a corner. She has dirty yellow fingers holding a cigarette to her wrinkly mouth. They turn and run back upstairs and into the room, collapsing together on a bed.

Amanda buries herself inside the funny-smelling blanket and feels the heat wrap around her. When she wakes up, Aunty Pammy has gone. She will be back in the morning, Barbara tells them.

'Come on then,' she says. They leave Tommo in the bed, one arm across his face, eyelids fluttering. In the kitchen she takes teabags, sugar and milk out of a Woolworth's bag and fills a kettle, eventually lights the cooker, then sits and waits. Amanda sits beside her and Jamie stands looking out the window.

'Beans on toast okay?' Barbara says. Before they can answer, the door opens and bickering voices spill in as the skeleton woman they saw by the stairs walks in with a gang of shabby children. She sits by Barbara and lights another cigarette. The kids fan out around her. A tall man strides in and sits down at the table.

'Hello all,' he says as he reaches for the woman's cigarette packet.

Barbara looks at him in surprise. He waves a few fingers at Amanda and she picks up her chair and moves nearer to her mum.

'Pass me the ashtray,' the woman says to him, and blows a thick stream of smoke over them all.

One of the little kids, a little boy of five or six, pulls on her arm.

'I'll swing for you in a bloody minute,' she tells him, and he stops and looks at Amanda and grins. 'You can use this cupboard,' she says to Barbara. 'You'll have to free up a bit of space in one of the fridges. I'd try that one first, the other one is on its last legs. How are you doing?' she says, looking from Barbara to Amanda and back.

Her mother shrugs her shoulders. Amanda mimics her. Barbara makes a cup of tea and when she has finished, the man gets up and does the same for himself and his mother, who sits picking at the bright red remains of polish speckling her nails. The manager comes into the room, her keys jingling against her hip.

'Perhaps Amanda and Jamie would like to explore the garden? We need to go over a few things.' The woman takes their mother away and they are left with these strangers, with this strange man who stares at Amanda as he smokes. The little boy comes over and says he'll show them outside.

Amanda moves away from him and stands behind Jamie, one hand on his shoulder as if they were posing for a school photograph. Even when the haggard-looking woman and the man leave, with the other kids scurrying after them like ducklings, they stay where they are, silent and still.

When Barbara finally comes back to the kitchen, she makes them beans on toast and fried eggs, and sits opposite her and Jamie as they all eat. Every time Amanda swallows the food it struggles to go down and then seems to have to go around a rock in her stomach. After a few bites she is done and her mum says nothing at all about the uneaten food. Barbara takes them to the residents' lounge, where they sit at the back of the room, unable to hear or see much of anything of the TV.

The man and his mother are there again. The mother is talking to a woman in a bright pink headscarf that matches her lips. She is drinking from a mug that has bright pink kisses all over it and a shirt that is stained. 'Never believe he was fifteen, would you?'

'Only fifteen? Well I never,' the headscarf woman says, and lifts a cigarette with a pink tip to her mouth.

Amanda is amazed. He is the same age as her brothers but twice the size of them. He towers over Jamie and has traces of a moustache.

'What are you in for?' he says to Jamie, and laughs.

'What?'

'Nowt.'

He stands really close to Amanda's chair until his leg touches hers.

'When I was a toddler and my dad came home pissed, he threw me in the air like he was playing, but when I came back down he punched me. He bust my lips open.' His face is smiling as he says this and he stares right at her without blinking.

'Mum. Muuuum,' she says.

Barbara looks round from where she is sitting, sees him hovering and motions for them to go to her.

The headscarf woman turns her bruised face to Barbara. 'Yous will all want your coats. It's bloody freezing in here.'

'I want to go to the room,' Amanda says.

'Go out and play, lovie,' the bony-faced woman says. 'Danny, take them outside.'

The little boy pops up from the side of a chair and grabs Amanda's hand. She feels too old, at almost ten, to play with such a little kid but she wants to leave the room so she allows herself to be led outside though Jamie frowns and sits himself down by Barbara. They walk down through the trees to the edge of the wall. It reminds her of the selfish giant's garden that someone, she thinks possibly Gran, read to her, long ago. The little boy pulls out a scrunched up cigarette from his pocket, lights it and takes a drag then offers it to her. Amanda takes a few puffs and is immediately dizzy, a wonderful, floaty feeling that makes the branches of the trees spin above her. She sits down on the grass and savours the feeling, closing her eyes until the feeling begins to recede. She holds her hand out for the cigarette again but he has already finished it. She places one hand against the wall and sees pinpricks of red, pitching around her splayed fingers. They are tiny spiders that move around like dodgem cars, running and reversing, changing direction every second. She lifts a finger and watches them run into the space where it was. Then she presses her finger down on top of the hectic little creatures and squashes them. When she pulls it up again, the dots have become a single red line. She repeats this, over and over, until there is a big blotchy smudge of red that almost covers the stone slab. And then she thinks of what she's just done; of the spider families that might be looking for each other in the devastation, that will never see each other again, the living creatures that she has destroyed. She gets up and runs back to the house, leaving the little boy calling after her. She goes into the old, cold toilet by the kitchen and washes the murder off her red-stained fingers in the chipped sink. And then she returns to the lounge where she sees Jamie kicking at the wall by the door.

'I want to go home,' he says.

Barbara glares at him. 'You can stop that for a start.'

'I want to go home. It's a fucking tip here.'

'Don't you dare swear,' she says, but gets up from the middle of a cloud of smoke, her hands moving constantly across her skirt, smoothing out the miniscule creases in the fabric.

'I'm tired out,' she says to no one specifically, 'we'll see you in the morning.'

Upstairs, Tommo is awake and eats the bread and butter their mum feeds him. Jamie bounces around on Amanda's bed but soon gives up and sits on the edge. They all stink of smoke as if they've just emerged from a bonfire. She thinks about what the man-boy said about 'what are you in here for' and she looks out of the window at the gates that now have a huge chain and padlock across them, locking them all inside together. She wants to leave, but she could never climb those walls and she feels her ribs tightening as if all the air is being pushed out and she opens her mouth and retches and out jerks a bit of food to sit on her skirt. She can't breathe at all, she is panting to try and get some air in and then something like an explosion happens in her head and she is all movement, her legs drumming the floor and her own hands, tightly fisted, hammer against her head. Her mum tries to pin her arms down and as she fights back they begin scuffling on the bed. She screams then, but it is a small sound, from the back of her mouth and though it goes on for a long time, it never gets louder. Her mum sits patting her shoulder as she cries, and when she is calmed, she leaves her sat between her brothers and brings her a glass of water from the kitchen. The glass is greasy and slides around in her palms. They all try smiling at each other and her mother's smile is wide as she reaches into her bag for one of her pills. Jamie gets into bed with Tommo and lies whispering to him and she curls up with her mum, listening to all the noises being made by unseen things, odd little skitterings that are relentless. She wants the toilet but is afraid to leave her bed, to walk down that long, dark corridor alone. She thinks she can hear the mice rattle around, hears tiny things dropping inside the walls. She is worried that they'll get out when she is asleep. They might jump on her face or bite her. One by one, her mum and her brothers fall asleep around her. She is left alone in the dark, listening to the sounds gathering at the foot of her bed, feeling her heart pumping in her ribs like a prisoner rattling the bars.

Part Five
Giving up the Ghost

Back for some more, eh? Okay, here goes. Do you know that I share my birthday with Shirley Temple? Hollywood's little darling. My mum and dad were both born in July. And my brothers share the same birthday, obviously. Dad used to tease me, when he was in a good mood, he'd say, 'You're the milkman's kid, that's why you have a birthday all alone.' I used to cry but now I wish I was the milkman's kid – I'd be over the fucking moon.

Why don't I just go to school? How fucking thick are you? I kept trying to go to school. I did go when I was at primary but I went mad and had to see a shrink. And then we left home and they tried putting me in another one near the hostel but I got sick from not sleeping and could never keep my breakfast down, so the doctor said I didn't have to go. And when we came back home I went on a trial to the Catholic middle school. I was supposed to stay there a week but the girls that used to pick on me were all there so I missed the bus the last two days and the shrink said I shouldn't go back to that school. I had to wait months until they decided if I could go to the local one or not and I loved it then because I stayed at Granny's every day, just waiting and playing cards and watching snooker with her and she'd always make me sandwiches for lunch with lemon barley water in a dark green glass and I used to think it tasted different to when it was in a white glass. I didn't get in until halfway through the year and everyone knew everyone and I was always feeling knackered so sometimes I'd just stop at the garages down the hill and mess about there instead. Or I'd get up late and walk up by the farm or to the reservoir with Bonnie. Always different schools, different kids, different teachers, everyone looking at me, the new girl, all the time, rubbing my skin off with their scratchy eyes. What do I mean by that? I can't explain what that means if you don't get it. It's just how it felt.

What fucking good is school anyway? There's no one wants me there, as per fucking usual, except for Mr K, and he just feels sorry for me because he's nice to everyone. Or in my case, every*thing*. I saw him pick up a worm once off the path behind the gym and he put it in the middle of the grass where he said it had a fighting chance. When I turned up late for school the first time, the headmistress asked me why, and when I said I'd got up late she was really angry and said they shouldn't have let me in that school, that I was bad news. And Mr fucking Adams... when he caught me fighting that girl, he didn't even want to know that she had started it by calling me a Paddy bastard; he just grabbed my shoulders and said right into my face they should lock me up because I was a thug. He hates me and I fucking hate him.

Do you know what school taught me? It taught me that everything I thought beautiful is just a lie, that the world is even uglier than me. I used to love art. Mrs Williams showed some pictures she said were famous the world over. In one of them the women had no clothes on and loads of lads whistled and everyone laughed, but I was looking at this painting of a rabbit. It was so good. It looked as if it would start moving about any second. But then she told us the paint was stuck to the canvas with glue made from boiled rabbits. I'm not fucking lying. She said they cook them into glue and then they put the glue on the cloth and then they paint on it. And she said all the colours are made from things like burned animal bones or ground-up insects or ink from dead fish. And they use animal hair in the brushes too. I told you it was mad. Using dead animal hair to dip into dead animals to make an illusion of that same animal. She said I was to stop being so silly but it's true. All those shadows and lights and lovely colours, even better than real life, but it's all from death. The only way I'm ever going to do any more fucking art is if I make a collage of me with all this skin dust and that pile of hair by the radiator. Use the dead bits of me to give an illusion of me being alive.

It's the same with music. I loved music until I started music class. I was always playing that tape Mr K gave me. And when Dad left I snuck his record player upstairs because Mum wouldn't let me play any of their wedding LPs, so I'd sing along in my room. Jim Reeves, the Mamas and the Papas and Simon and Garfunkel. And a Miles Davis one. Mum told me once that one of her friends had given it them as a wedding present but that Dad had called it 'blackie voodoo music' so she hid it under her old coat at the bottom of her bed box. I couldn't stop playing that one. It didn't seem to start or end, just notes and notes, and you couldn't stop listening because you were trying to catch them all in your head. Every time I listened it was different, like some notes had disappeared and new ones had turned up instead. I think he might have been crazy, making music like that. Crazy music for a crazy fucking pig-girl. I wish I'd just listened to the sounds instead of having music *education*. Strings made from guts, drums from skin, pipes and keys from bones and teeth. And saxophones and trumpets and those what-do-you-call-its, clarinets – they collect spit every time you play them. It makes me heave to even think of it. I tried and tried not to think how they're making the music, but I could see it all in my head, a heap of dead animals without skin or teeth and half their bones missing. I don't listen to it anymore. Not even my teacher's tape.

In science we did all about how plants grow. I couldn't get enough of it at the start: all the different types in the world and every one of them able to live by just sucking the heat out of the sun. And they shine in a million shades, a never ending blend of greens, reds, blues, purples, yellows, whites and even golds and silvers. But all those pretty flowers and plants and fruit and that, they live on shit and rot and then we eat it all up. Disgusting. They kill each other to get more space to grow. And they're cannibals. Cabbages will eat other cabbages, beans will eat other beans. Jesus, if you cut a rose off a bush and throw it at the roots, it will eat itself. I stopped going to that class, I didn't want to know anymore. And sex education. Jesus Christ. I'm not going to be caught out that way. No fucking chance. You can catch diseases that make your bits rot. There was this guy's, you know, prick, that was all deformed, like a cauliflower. I fucking hate being a girl. Yeah, I know. I know I'm not a girl, I know I'm not even fucking human, but I'm supposed to be a girl and I don't like that. Some of the girls at school were always talking about sprogs, always babbling about how cute their sister's or their cousin's or their neighbour's baby is and how they like to cuddle them and how they want one, in a bit. Who'd want that? Something alive inside you, like a parasite? It makes me feel sick. I'm not going to be a bloody storage facility for some little alien that will grow up to hate me anyway.

These girls at school walk around covered in make-up, and when I tell them they look like they're not real, like paintings, and it's death and suffering they've smeared on themselves, they don't get it. Mum and Aunty Pammy are the same, never without lipstick and perfume, even to church. I told them what that animal rights lad with the stall in Rochdale showed me, that lipstick is just pig fat and perfume is made with stuff out of deer's bums and that it's all tested on animals, but they just said they didn't think so. But it's true. He showed me all these pictures of monkeys and cats with things in their brains. He told me about it all, about animal experiments and the army shooting live pigs and all sorts. He told me about fur and leather and silk as well and I showed Mum the leaflets he gave me but she just said I wasn't to talk to him again and chucked them in the bin. I told her I don't want to walk around in dead animals and she was furious because she'd just bought me some new school shoes. Not that shoes matter anymore, not where I am.

School was a nightmare, except for English. That was the only class I went to all of last year. I'd just go in twice a week, two hours, for English. We read *The Day of the Triffids*, which was a great story but a bit young for me. After that it was *The Chrysalids*, which was brilliant. I know what it's like hiding your true self from people because you're all deformed and if they see it they'll fucking torment you or murder you. I could write any stuff I wanted to in English, anything at all, Mr Kramm said. But the rest of the time there were too many questions – teachers, kids, dinner ladies, the caretaker – all asking me why I was wasting my brains. I couldn't find any of my own words for all of theirs filling my head. And when that happened, there was fuck all left for me. Domestic science was cooking dead animals. History is full of fights. Geography is where they did the fights. They made me piss around like a knob in drama but they said I'd fallen too far behind to do French anymore, even though I knew my fucking verb tenses better than anyone in that class. They put me down a class in maths and all, and it was stuff a baby could do that bored me rigid. I hated woodwork and the chemistry teacher hated me and used to say things about me being a waste of space in front of the whole fucking class until I had to get out. And who wants to run round a fucking field or after a netball with dickhead lads shouting abuse at you? Shirley fucking Temple, eh? That's me to a tee, Mum and Dad's little darling.

．ం

We keep going round in circles. You think this world is so fantastic? It's a shit tip. It is proof of hell, right here on earth. I used to think meat tasted delicious. But it was alive once so when you eat that stuff you're eating veins and skin and blood. It's disgusting. Cakes are full of eggs, which are hens' periods, and sweets are made with gelatine, which is the goo in the middle of bones. Everything we eat is disgusting. Sometimes I imagine all the germs crawling over the food Mum gives me and I can't even touch it.

I told Mum I don't want to eat meat and I gave her a list of things that I want to eat: bananas, oven chips, apples, oranges, baked beans, crisps, chocolate, oranges, biscuits, toast, black coffee, water, cordial, pop. Oh, and potatoes – baked or roasted but not mashed. I love potatoes so don't tell me anything horrible about them, I don't want to know. I also told her what makes me feel sick: dead animals of any kind, gravy (made from blood), eggs, pears and tomatoes (seeds look like insects), melted cheese (looks like sick), milk or custard or yoghurt (sticks in my throat), bread (too squidgy and makes my mouth go funny). She said okay but she still gives me fish fingers or crispy pancakes almost every night. Dad used to say there's no meat in that shit anyway. Now I eat it with my left hand so I can pull my hair with my right and then I don't think about what's in it.

I live in my own dirt and filth, but you're all the same, living among rat-infested heaps of rubbish, polluting the planet. We're all just slimy skin-bags full of dirt; piss and shit and germy spit, boils and blackheads and earwax and snot and that stuff you have to poke out of the corners of your eyes. We're constantly spreading viruses and diseases, passing on TB or measles or polio or cholera. Every time we go to the toilet we can infect each other. I try not to go at all. We leave bits of ourselves all over the place; hairs and skin and sweaty, greasy trails, like slugs. Hands leave invisible bacteria smears and it burrows in through your pores and your stomach churns and your bum explodes in a sea of stinking sickness. People blast out microbes with every cough and sneeze and they sail up your nostrils and drip out of your nose and eyes. We have to clean ourselves constantly because of the infectious mess we've got inside us. It makes me sick.

When we're not busy contaminating each other with poxes, we're blowing bits off one other in a thousand different wars, filling the world with bullets and bombs. Russia and America are going at it right now, showing off their nuclear arsenals and threatening to blow each other to fuck and the world with them. I watched a documentary about it a year or so back. It showed pictures of deformed babies in Japan where they dropped bombs. Mum shouted at me when she saw me watching it, told me to stop worrying about things that I can't do anything about. Told me to go switch it over and then she went back to reading her stupid magazine with all the women stood around in dresses, and their arms and legs bent all weird like they're practising for a game of Twister.

And the world is full of people like my dad, always ready and waiting to crush anyone into a bloody pulp, to batter or torment or abuse. There are worse people than my dad out there, so bad they make us look like the fucking Waltons. Do you know there are serial killers roaming America that have never been caught? I saw a programme about that as well. It was on late at night, after Mum had gone to bed. It said at any one time there are hundreds and hundreds of them, walking around waiting to pounce. There must be serial killers here too. All across the world there are whole masses of people with their wickedness bubbling away under the rules and regulations, waiting for the rulers to change so they can do their bidding, Nazis or Commies or Fascists – or even fucking Tories letting soldiers shoot kids dead in Belfast with rubber bullets. I can feel it in the air when I go out, the rage and hatred, like the devil's breath, poisoning people until they do things that you and I can't even imagine. I don't want to go outside into that. I want to stay here where they can't get me.

Look at that! An old fag, stuck between the radiator pipes. Course I'm going to smoke it! Mum only brought me five up tonight because they're all coming in the morning and she'll get in trouble. I'll have this old one now and save the new ones for later, when it's gone dark. I don't have to smoke it in thirds to make it last, for a change, I can smoke the whole thing in one go. I'll just spit on my jeans after to get the aftertaste of it out of my gob, like I do when I've run out of fags and have to smoke all the dog ends. It will taste bloody disgusting but I'll still get all dizzy if I have three drags really fast and that's the main thing.

I'm so fucking sick of thinking all the time. I can't make sense of anything and I can't sleep at night, lying under a blanket with the light blazing in my eyes because I daren't switch it off, waiting for morning to come and all these thoughts to leave me alone. I used to daydream, you know, I used to spend whole nights pretending I had a different life; pretty face and nice clothes and a shiny black pony and a red Capri that I have a special licence to drive and everyone at school watching me and wanting to be my friend. Now I can't be arsed. I try not to think about where Jamie and Tommo are and what might have happened to them and why they've not come back to see me or why Mum fell out with Aunty and Gran and Grandad and why did I have to go nuts like this and why couldn't I have been a favourite to either Mum or Dad, why did they both have to like Jamie and Tommo best and if I couldn't be Dad's favourite why did he have to hate me *so* much. I try not to think about all the bad in the world and how it's extinguising the tiny little bit of good, flattening it until it ends up like an old car squashed into a cube and then what will happen to us all when the bomb goes off. It's all inside my head so that when I sleep, I have all these dreams about war and murder and being trapped in the house with my dad or I'm in a prison and the door has no keyhole. I remember this one nightmare where Dad was beating Tommo and me and Jamie were trying to stop him but he just kicked at us to keep us away. And then Dad had disappeared but we could hear Tommo shouting for us to help him, and when we opened the pantry door, Dad's walking stick was upside down and Tommo's head was stuck onto the end. I can still see that in my mind. Now I keep having the same one, night after night, about one of the paintings my teacher showed me of someone yelling on a bridge. She said it's called *The Scream*, and in my dream it wakes up and starts screeching and screeching right in my face and I keep trying to understand what it wants me to do. I'm tired all of the time because I can't sleep even when I'm sleeping, and when I wake up and climb out of bed my head is heavy from all the stuff in my dreams. Sometimes I'm so tired I'm not even sure if I've slept or if I'm dreaming awake, because when I'm tired and I shut my eyes all these memories flash up. My mind is like a fucking camera, taking all these pictures of malformed babies and clubbed seal pups, the orange flash of an A-bomb and the unstoppable crawl of disease over skin, Dad shouting, the walking stick raised in his hand, his fist ramming into Tommo's nose or Jamie's eye, Tommo not being able to walk or speak when we got to the hostel, just sitting there watching us with his eyes all shaky. And my memory is the fucking photo album, shuffling the images and pushing them out at random.

Jesus, I wish I was thick. Ignorance really is bliss. Hard to think too much when you can't think at all. If you think about fear, it wraps itself around you like a cape. Sometimes I wish I could just end it. End it all. I know you're thinking that's what I should do. If I knew that dying was the finish, just rotting in the ground and it's all over, nothing more to live through, I'd do it. Right now. I wouldn't even have to hack at myself with this bit of mirror. I could just pop next door and get Mum's sleeping pills out of the bathroom cabinet and swallow the fucking lot. Maybe she's left them there hoping I'll top myself. No more pain in the arse for poor, tired old Mum. But what if there is something after death? I'm not that scared of hell – I reckon the queue's going to be a fucking long one, what with Hitler and Pol Pot and all the murderers and rapists, not to mention Dad right up at the head of the queue.

But what if there is no heaven or hell but no nothingness either? What if killing yourself changes nothing? I read about Buddhism in Tommo's encyclopaedia and it said you just keep coming back. So what if killing yourself wasn't an escape? What if it just shunts you into another piss-poor life? Or worse, what if it all just carries on exactly the same because you killed yourself? You end up back where you started, all over again. None of us have any fucking clue what death is or where we'll end up, and that scares me. I'll just have to wait until this fat carcass of mine stops breathing all by itself. Gran told me a few years back about her friend Winnie who died. I asked if she was sick and she said, 'No, love. She'd just given up the ghost.' Well, look at me, white as a sheet, living with the bugs in the fucking shadows. I'm a ghost. And I'm giving up.

Part Six
When it was good
for a while

．

They are back home but it's as if Amanda has forgotten
how it used to be. It's not the same now, it feels smaller and
tighter. Dad has painted up the rooms and bought lots of new
furniture for her and her brothers' bedrooms. Everything is
over-bright, like someone else's house, so she runs around
the house looking for familiar things. She hates the yellow
lump of a dressing table and the bright pink bedspread which
sit next to each other like misshapen fondant fancies. She
finds her old school shoes and her wellingtons in the new
wardrobe that she no longer minds being cream. Neither of
them fit anymore, they pinch at the toes. She tries on her
old blue T-shirt and it seems okay but her old trousers leave
her ankles poking out and she can't button them. There is a
small cupboard under the mirror with a door that opens with
a neat click. She likes to listen to the small sound it makes
as it opens and closes. She also likes to move her clothes
around in the matching chest of drawers, so that for a day the
first drawer is full, then for a day it is the turn of the middle
drawer and then the third. The fourth contains her socks and
knickers and she lets them lie there because there are too
many little bundles to move easily. She pokes her finger into
the small hole in the skirting board that has been painted
the same cream and is still slightly sticky to the touch. She
sees the same bit of raggedy carpet at the back of the new
television that Bonnie chewed once, and the barrel-shaped
spoons at breakfast with *Made in Sheffield* stamped on their
handles. She laughs when she sees the scuffs on the inside

of the table leg that she made trying to kick her brothers when they had to sit there until they ate up their dinners. She likes to walk from the front room or the kitchen to her room because Dad doesn't yell if she does and she no longer gets out of breath from too many stairs.

Father Quinn brought them home in his car. Seamus came running to meet them. He stood hopping from one foot to the other with his hands making box-like shapes in the air in front of them as he tried to hug her brothers. In the end, as they backed away down the path, he dropped his hands down and gave them all awkward handshakes, one by one, as if they were being introduced for the first time. His mouth was so full of words that he ended up gabbling, sounding a little like a turkey as he ran around putting a pot of tea and a plate of chocolate fingers and digestives on the table. He clasped Tommo's hands and Tommo leaped backwards as if electrocuted, but Seamus just patted him on the shoulder and waved his arm at the table, also littered with Pacer mints and Spangles and tubes of Toffos. There were crisps in bowls and a tiny heap of pink Anglo bubbly next to a stack of comics. He physically curled their fingers round glasses of lemonade, smiling all the time like Willy Wonka. He took their mum's arm by the elbow as if leading her for a dance, seating her at the table and then grabbing her hands and collapsing against her bosom like a baby, crying while they stood around him trying not to look.

'No more,' he kept saying, looking at each of them with red eyes, 'no more.'

After a while, her dad began to make his old jokes. Soaked in sugar, she laughed along with her dad and with Tommo and Jamie and when she saw that her mum wasn't making any noise she laughed for her, the noise high and sharp like a coin scraped over stone.

'Haven't I told you to help yourself – to anything,' he says every now and again waving his arm over the bread bin, the fruit bowl, the biscuit barrel. Amanda is stuffed with sweets, but takes something every time he offers. She has chocolate biscuits jammed in her jeans pockets, melting into the warm cloth.

Gran and Grandad pop round, all smiles and hugs and handing out pound notes. 'For the sake of the kids,' she hears Gran say when she is helping Mum wash up. Aunty Pammy sits at the opposite corner without speaking to Dad and he passes round a plate of biscuits before placing the plate in front of her with a grin right across his face. She ignores it and tells Amanda what a good girl she is and sits her on her knee while she makes a big fuss of the boys. Amanda is too big and perches awkwardly, trying not to fall off, her aunty's bony knees poking into the back of her legs.

Seamus comes home, early one Saturday morning, with two, tiny baby rabbits that he says Amanda can keep. When she asks where they're from, he says they dropped out of the sky, and she blots out her thoughts of the hunting, pushes away the images of limp dead bodies, blood pouring from an eye or an ear, hanging down next to his gun. She carries them around with her all weekend, cradling and kissing them. She begs her mum to let them sleep with her but she is told that she might squash them and anyway their business would get everywhere so she keeps them in a box in the new wooden shed her dad has built. He comes home one afternoon after work with a hutch and Amanda carefully places a margarine tub full of water and a pile of dandelion leaves just behind the mesh screen. She runs down every few minutes to look at the soft grey ovals nestling in the straw. She is called to the house by her mum and sees the kitchen full of people. She recognises the lady who came when she was little, who pulled at all her clothing and didn't tuck it back in afterwards. The lady's hair is grey at the sides now. Seamus takes the lady and a man who is with her around the house and he tells Amanda to come too. He shows the people his handiwork: the new red flock wallpaper in the front room, the newly painted walls in every room, her brothers' new bunk beds, solid and gleaming, with a ladder up to the top bed. When they go back down, Amanda shows them her brand new post office set that she found at the end of her bed when she first came home.

When the boys get back from their paper rounds, Seamus tells them to bring their new calculators and they race up the stairs. The people then leave. The man shakes Seamus' hand as he stands proud in front of them, the blue stripes on his Sunday shirt flashing in the sunlight coming through the window. The lady is already at the gate. Amanda runs to the end of the garden and hears her say, 'A leopard never changes its spots,' and Amanda imagines how it would look if they could, all striped like zebras or patchy like giraffes. She waves bye to the woman who waves back and then disappears inside her car.

And she's not had to stay, after all, at the the big Catholic school, where she knows the girls would have been waiting. She reads all the letters sent by the education board, addressed to her father but opened by her mother, stashed in the sideboard on top of the old gas and electricity bills. Unlike her brothers she doesn't have to join the queue of black uniforms waiting for their buses. She finally wears the new, blue uniform of the local school and because she missed so much of the year they give her tests to do and she is put in the top sets anyway. It is much nearer to home and as she walks in with two girls from the top of the street. She times it every day on her new watch and notes the times in her diary with a lock on the front. It is between 7 minutes and 36 seconds and 9 minutes and 3 seconds, depending how late they are. The school is small but the fifth and sixth formers are huge and when these giant hordes pour out of the exits at home time, as if the school has sprung leaks on all sides, she tries to push ahead, desperate to avoid being sucked into the middle of that surge.

She knew on her very first day that she would have to scrap her way into the school rankings. She has been there four days when Roberts, the cock of the yard, comes over to her in the playground with a gangly mob of lads in tow.

'I really like you,' he says, loudly, grinning all the time at his mates.

'Fuck off.'

'I mean it, I really like you. Give us a kiss.'

'Go fuck yerself. Leave me alone.'

She tries to walk through them, but they close ranks and she finds herself in the middle of a mass of faces. Roberts steps forward, his mouth pursed into fish lips, and he grabs her and pulls her towards him smacking his lips in the air. She can hear the tittering as she tries to get free, her long hair getting caught in the button of his jacket. She turns suddenly, so quickly that he is still kissing the air. She throws his arm off her and jumps up high into the air, reaching for his head. His hair is short so she locks her fingers round his ears and twists her hands, jerking his head to the right. His fists are wheeling, striking her again and again in the face. She kicks him hard as she can behind the kneecap. Unbalanced, he trips and falls and then she wades in, pulling his head up and punching him right in his face. She sees a teacher running towards them just before the crowd gathers, clamouring, moving in ever closer in their need for second-hand pleasure. Hands clutch at her jumper, stretching it in every direction, pulling her tie until it shrinks into a small, hard knot. She sees his mate move in. He lands a blow at the top of her head so she lets go of Roberts and grabs his fringe and meets his lowering head with her knee. Roberts is already back on his feet, though he stands there doing nothing. She pushes and pushes at the stiff heave of arms and elbow until she smacks straight into Mr Adams.

'Don't think I didn't see who started that, you little hooligan.'

He drags her off to the headmistress' office where she is asked to explain herself and to apologise and to promise that this will not be the way she will repay the chance they've given her in letting her into the school. But she feels at peace. It is over, her reputation sealed. She is restarted, transformed, will be left alone now. She will never admit her relief that Mr Adams pushed his way in and dragged her out by the collar, that he was only just in time to stop the trembling that she could feel bubbling up as the hands of the crowd seemed to reach right inside her head. She doesn't care that Mr Adams told her as he marched her along that he has the measure of her, that he wouldn't let any bloody Irish into his school if he had his way. She has no need to tell anyone she thought she was losing, that she was sinking under the relentless assault. She saw all the eyes on her, the girl that fought the hard boys, as she was pulled across the school grounds.

She is at school, in the hot, airless squash of bodies, for 7 hours and 15 minutes. Depending on the day, she traces the movements of British armies for an hour or solves quadratic equations or writes up chemical processes in wallpaper-covered books. She then goes with her three newest friends to smoke behind the gym, then to PE or RE or DT before eating her lunch. She then pushes her way through the afternoon, fifty minutes filing a small piece of metal that will be a key ring or baking iced buns or drawing a collection of fruit on a coloured cloth. Another break where she heads to smokers' corner to join the gang of desperately puffing mouths while eyes are all peeled for teachers. Then the last class of the day, thank Jesus, where she sketches the leaves of plants or watches the green letters flash on a tiny little computer that the teacher with the handlebar moustache is demonstrating to the class. Unless it's last thing on Wednesdays and Fridays, because then she sits in her favourite class with her favourite teacher, writing poems and stories that only he reads. Words spring up from somewhere deep it's like she's slipped into a well inside of her; she writes words she will never use at home or with the few friends she has at school or on her street, words without accent, spoken only by dictionaries or her almanacs. She writes of missing her brothers and the myth of love or freedom. She never times those classes. And then she is moving homewards again.

Seamus plays the 'baiting' game almost daily after work, throwing pretend punches around, rubbing his knuckles hard against the back of their heads, pinching them on the undersides of their upper arms until they shout out with pain. Then they lie around together to watch Harold Lloyd on BBC2. Her dad makes funny faces at her all the time and even though she knows she is too old, she plays along because she doesn't want his face to change.

He is constantly joking with them. They have a little routine where they ask, 'What's for tea, Dad?' and he replies, 'Black man's diarrhoea,' and they laugh while Mum scolds him for being disgusting.

When they return from church on Sundays, they join Dad in the front room where he is playing his Irish records and Amanda and her brothers are allowed a single glass of homebrew mixed with lemonade. The shandy is sweet and sour at the same time and she wants to drink it all down but she sips, trying to make it last. They sit there singing along with him and Amanda knows when the songs get rude because Mum giggles and goes red but doesn't know exactly why. Mum refuses to listen to Dad's Irish rebel songs album and goes to make the dinner as soon as it comes out. Dad now talks to them at the dinner table and Jamie and Tommo join in but Amanda's words feel strange here, loud and crowded up against her face. She feels like she is talking another language so she listens instead, watching first one jolly face and then another. She watches her mum's slender hands working, cutting meat or raising a forkful of roast potato or a glass of water to her mouth and when Amanda smiles, her mum smiles back, and Amanda knows that her grandad would say that smiles are the one thing never rationed.

One Wednesday, after breakfast, their dad holds a set of tickets in the air. Just over an hour later they're on the terraces at Old Trafford with a new scarf and bag apiece. Amanda hops around on the terrace to keep warm and wishes Mum had let her wear trousers.

'Can we cheer, Dad?' Jamie asks.

'Go right ahead.'

They start hesitantly.

'Yeah,' they say, quietly at first. After a few minutes they shout again, a bit louder,

'Yeah – YEAHHHHHH.' They egg each other to shout more and more. Then Amanda shouts.

'Wooooooooshhhhh,' like Dad does when he watches on the TV at home, though the players are nowhere near the goal. The people around them laugh.

'Go on, son,' yells Jamie and everyone laughs even harder.

By half-time their voices are raw, broken. Even the players look up, grinning, as they jog towards the tunnel. When they appear again for the second half, Amanda and her brothers clap and cheer and jump up and down. And old man turns round, his face a mass of wrinkles under a smooth flat cap, and smiles.

'Calm down, eh? It's only the reserves,' he says. 'I'll be deaf as a post by the time it ends.'

The sparse crowd turn round and laugh and Amanda and her brothers laugh right back with them.

'Talk to my kids once more and I'll fucking drop you.'

All faces swivel towards their dad. The old man looks at him and then moves away, limping as he does. Some of the others around them whisper to each other. All of them look back at the match.

'Go on,' he tells them, spreading his arms wide but it's as if the game has already finished and they are back to the tame calls that they started with. After the match they eat pie and chips from the shop at the ground and they go home with bellies full and she is half carried home when they get off the train because she is so sleepy. She can't remember going to bed but wakes up with her scarf under her pillow.

Amanda feels the air around her sparking, tiny needles pricking at the back of her neck. She can hear it though her brothers laugh at her when she asks them about it; it makes the same noise the sky does just before a storm. Every time she laughs or her mum lets a plate ring against the steel of the draining board or Tommo and Jamie bicker upstairs she looks at her dad to see what he is doing. She tries to keep guard, tries to watch everyone do everything.

She sees her mother silent most of the time, drumming her nails against her tea mug. She sees her dad's smile clamped tight across his face as if he has glued it there, sees his fingers curl into almost-fists before he stretches them instead and cracks his knuckles. She saw him slide into the outhouse once, heard objects shatter as they hit the bricks. Bonnie still won't go near him. Since they got back, the dog moves in a strange new way whenever Dad appears, slithering, snake-like, across the floor. Sometimes she yelps if he gets near her and then she backs up against the wall and squashes what she can of her little barrel body into the space between the fridge and the wall. Amanda has to move constantly to stop the feeling that she is going to fall, jostling her legs against the sofa frame, picking at the tiny threads on the tablecloth, rubbing her fingers together until they burn as if blistered. If the fizzing in her stomach gets bad she has to relieve herself. Sometimes she has time to run to the toilet or if she is outside, the side of a field or the underneath of a privet bush, but occasionally she vomits right where she stands.

Amanda is longing for Christmas. She is tired of sneaking past the staff room so she can sit in a cubicle in the toilets by the gym instead of going to Mr Adam's geography class and not able to move or speak a word in case he pounces on her and berates her in front of the class; another Dad in a different shirt. She is having problems staying in any of her classes. She prefers the toilets with their sharp, disinfectant stink. The lavatory rim blocks that look like circles of mint cake have her eyes watering even when she's put all the lids down. Her nose still detects the faint stench of piss underneath. Better to sit there, getting increasingly dizzy than watching classroom walls moving in on her. If the smell of shit hits her when she opens the door she creeps instead, along the outer wall of the fifth-year unit and runs past the tennis courts and over the wall and around by the farm fields. She hates all the smells of school, the reek of farts or feet, the bitter smell of unwashed armpits, the mustiness of damp uniforms, the mixed up food smells wafting from the dining hall that makes her retch and think of cabbage and custard and gravy and meat pie all slopping together on a thick white plate. She can smell her own armpits, she is sure, as she sits fidgeting in her seat, can feel the damp beads forming as she is hemmed in on all sides by bodies, all with their own smell adding to the soupy odour hanging like a cloud under the ceiling. She hates having to sit in a chair that so many others have sat in, at a desk with oily fingertip smudges shining among the penned and scratched-in graffiti. She can't bear the constant chattering, can almost see the germs in the spittle flying from all these lips.

She was hoping that Aunty Pammy would come today with her advent calendars but when she gets back the house is in uproar. Granny and Grandad are there and Granny is holding Bonnie on a lead. Amanda doesn't even answer their hellos but flies up the stairs calling for her mum. She finds her in the bedroom where a suitcase is again open, though the contents are neatly stacked. On Amanda's bed is a brand new outfit, blue jeans with red piping around the pockets and a white T-shirt with something written in big red letters on the front. When she reads *Skateboards rool ok?* she knows her dad has chosen it.

'What's going on?'

'Wait and see,' her dad says, appearing in the doorway with a mound of new underwear for the boys hanging over his arm. He seizes Amanda and pretends to jive with her until socks and underpants rain down onto the floor, their labels stuck up like parachutes. He scoops them up and carries on dancing, his feet tapping as he goes back into his bedroom. She repeats her question to her mum.

'Bring me a new soap down from the cistern,' her mum says as she goes back downstairs. By the time Amanda has dug one out from under the piles of sheets on the shelf, her brothers are also back home and talking ten to the dozen in the front room.

'Shut yer eyes,' their dad yells and when he gets just outside the front room. 'Are they shut?'

'Yes, Dad,' Jamie says when nobody else speaks.

'You can open them now.'

He is stood in a brand new black suit. Gold-coloured square cufflinks twinkle at the end of his sleeves and he has a red-and-blue tie on. He hands Jamie and Tommo their new clothes; navy cord trousers and long-sleeved red sweatshirts, and points to the green parkas hanging over the arms of the couch.

'Where are we going?' Tommo asks.

'To the ferry at Liverpool,' he says, 'come this time tomorrow, we'll all be home.'

Their Irish grandmother is a fat woman, much fatter than the few photos Amanda's seen and they show her as large enough. She is short, in a tent-like dress that balloons everywhere except in the middle, where it has tucked itself in under a thick roll around her stomach. They are all crushed inside the miniscule front room with a low roof and Irish Gran is stood in front of the narrow door frame hanging crookedly in the wall, which makes her look out of proportion, as if she lives in a funhouse. Her mum and dad are sat on the two chairs with various aunties and uncles perched on the arms. Others lean against the tiny table.

'Say hello to your granny,' her dad says.

The Irish grandmother looks at them with an unfriendly expression.

'Hello, Gran,' Tommo and Jamie say at the same time.

'Hello yourself,' she says. Only her mouth responds. Nothing else on her face moves a muscle.

'Hello, Gran,' Amanda says.

Her gran looks her up and down. 'Well, if it isn't Two-Ton-Tessie,' and she laughs so hard that she shakes like a jelly from top to bottom. Her uncles and aunties laugh. She stands there with her face hot with hate that is instant and strong. She turns her back and looks at her fingers as if she's remembered something she left on them.

'Go outside for a bit. Have a look around,' Barbara says, her voice as soft as Amanda has ever heard it. She looks up and sees her mother's face dark and angry as she stares at her Irish grandmother.

'Your cousins will be along now,' an aunty says. 'Just wait there, so.'

As Amanda and her brothers file out of the door she trips over the step and jostles her dad, whose hand shoots out automatically but only pinches her ear and then flops back down by his side.

They sit by the big metal gate.

'Don't worry about her,' Tommo says.

'I'm not. Anyway, she can fucking talk,' Amanda says. 'She's like a brick shithouse.'

'Like two brick shithouses knocked together,' Tommo says, and they all start giggling.

'She looks just like Dad – in a dress,' she says, and they all laugh out loud. She imagines him in the same faded floral dress, the same old cardigan with sagging pockets. The mild stench of cowpat floats across the road and they hold their noses up at each other and laugh. They hear laughs fired back at them as two boys and a girl in dirty T-shirts, coats and trousers come around the corner. They come right up to the gate.

'How-ya?' the tallest one says. 'We heard you were coming. I'm Liam. This here's Christie. She's Donna.' It turns out these are the cousins they are waiting on. Close on their heels comes a very short man with filthy, ripped trousers stuffed into old boots and a huge coat that reaches down to his knees. Rabbits dangle from both coat sleeves. He looks like he has dead rabbits for hands. He comes over grinning, showing crooked teeth and doesn't speak, just stands there, nodding and smiling. Liam moves behind him.

'Uncle Barney, yer a stupid fucking cunt,' he says.

Amanda is shocked. She looks at the man who has said nothing at all to this and she looks at her brothers who stare at Liam. The man notices their faces.

'Shut your fucking pie hole,' he growls at their cousin. Then he goes back to watching Tommo and Jamie and grinning.

Liam bends right down to his uncle's ear, and yells, 'Barney, you stupid fucker. Yer deaf old fucker.'

He begins to dance at the back of the oblivious man and she sees her brother pretending to cough. She doesn't want to laugh but she can't help herself. The man carries on walking around to the back of the cottage.

'Wanna go for a walk?' Christie says, sweeping his hand in the direction of the fields that stretch as far as the eye can see. Silver flashes from the thick frost.

The newly expanded band of Duffys marches off together to the long, green stretch of field at the side of the house. Amanda is happy to have a girl to tag along with for a change, even if the girl is three years younger. She links arms with Donna as they stride out over the long grass. The field is full of icy pats of dung and she's put both feet in it before they've got to the end. Her trainers will need washing. Her cousins are all in wellies. The next field is even bigger and right at the opposite end are a huge herd of brown and white cows. Unlike the ones at home, these all have long horns. She stands back as Liam pushes the gate as far as the old metal wire will allow it. They all file through but she hangs back, waiting until the last minute to squeeze herself through the tiny gap. They are about halfway across the field when the cows see them and come running over, hoping for food. Within minutes they are encircled.

'They belong to Old Ackie,' Donna says, smacking the nearest of the cows on the nose until they back up a little. Amanda is surrounded by wet nostrils blowing steam in her face. The cows have started making tiny grunting noises and butting at them, and she imagines falling under all those jigging hooves. A shot gun sounds with a huge bang that echoes in the air.

'Jeysus, he'll go fucking mad if he catches us in his field,' Liam says. He is pushing at the cows, trying to get them to move backwards.

Jamie and Tommo join the cousins in pushing the cows who groan and stamp around and slowly make room in the middle of them.

'Shoo dere, shoo dere,' Liam says. They all join in with him and then take off their coats and flap them at the cows' heads. Another gunshot sounds and another, and the cows get spooked and bang into each other as they try to move. As soon as a space clears, Liam starts running. Amanda races along the field with the others, the cows well ahead now, and she likes the new sensation in her throat, scorched with freedom and running and the cold air. There is no sign of the mad farmer, the shots haven't come again, and they slow as they near the edge of the meadow. The cows, however, don't stop. They keep running, breaking straight through the hedge, crushing the thorny bushes underfoot. They charge through the new hole in the hedge and go careening down the road.

'Fuck's sake,' Liam says. 'Come on.'

They run the full length of the hedgerow along the left-hand side and then Liam rolls himself over it, landing by the stretch of wood on the other side. Amanda puts her hands together, shoves Donna over and then does the same for Christie. Tommo does likewise for her and then him and Jamie vault over it, landing on the top and having to scramble over the hedge. They get to a clearing where they stop and sit on the damp mossy ground and start laughing.

'Those fucking cows, Jeysus, they'll be in fucking Dublin by now.'

'I hope nobody saw us, we'll be murdered,' Christie replies.

'I'm starving,' Tommo says. Amanda realises her own stomach is thumping. They walk through the woods until they see the road winding round again. They have to cross a ditch to get to the road, a deep stinking trench with a slimy log for crossing. Liam runs across and falls just at the edge, one foot in the swampy black water. He scrambles, cursing, up the bank. Amanda sits astride the log and drags herself across with her hands. It is slow going and when she gets to the other side her trousers and hands are covered in green-black muck, but she is merely damp, not drenched. Her brothers copy her and then likewise Donna and Christie, then they wait for Liam to get his bearings. They have run and walked for miles, he tells them, they have a good hour of walking to get home. They are tired and quiet and the jokes are finished.

It is almost dusk when they go back inside the cottage, but nobody asks where they've been. It stinks of whiskey and cigarettes and her dad is arguing with her uncle Sean. They face each other with lips drawn up around their teeth, like a couple of dogs, snapping at each other across the tiny table while their Irish gran sits grinning as if watching a comedy. Amanda hears something about what would happen if you put an Irish stamp on a letter and then posted it from England, but their voices are mixed with the rattly snores of another uncle, asleep on the sofa, whose name she hasn't been told as yet, the extremely ugly one with a huge red nose as dimpled and mottled as old orange peel. A woman staggers through the door in high heels, helped by her aunty Brigid, who is now heavily pregnant. She has on a silky red frock that looks like a splash of blood against the drab pale walls. Mascara has run down her face. She is speaking but she is so drunk the words drop from her mouth and Amanda can't make anything out.

'Ahh, Daddy, Daddy,' she suddenly wails and moves towards the tiny picture hung over the fireplace with arms outstretched. Aunty Brigid can't hold on to her though she tries, clutching her waist with both hands as if she were a rope in a tug of war. She almost falls on top of Barbara, but Seamus leaps up and drags her to her feet. Amanda watches her Irish gran cross the room and grab the woman by her hair as she droops between Seamus and Brigid. She hits her in the mouth, her knuckles big and bulging. The woman doesn't respond though blood shows on her bottom lip. Aunty Brigid finally gets her body in front of her sister.

'Mammy, don't.'

Seamus shrugs off his drunken sister's arm and leaves her collapsed against Brigid, who falters under the weight.

'Give me a hand with your mother,' she says to the cousins. Christie and Donna get up and manoeuvre their mother to the chair they've just vacated. Her gran sits back down with Seamus. Amanda bites her nails, sees Tommo and Jamie wringing their hands. Liam walks out of the room and returns with a plate piled high with buttered soda bread. As he kicks the door closed behind him, her own mother is revealed in the corner, grey smoke billowing around her as if she has just been conjured up. Amanda watches the pink-painted nail of her mother's finger as she taps the end of the cigarette into an ashtray, watches her face that is as calm as if they were sat in church.

'Sit yous down,' Liam says, and Amanda and her brothers move quickly to the battered seats. Amanda shares one with Donna, Tommo and Jamie share the other and Liam balances himself on the edge of the sofa. Christie settles himself on the floor. The bread is delicious, the butter is thick and creamy and they gobble the food down. Amanda holds up her filthy hands and shows them to her brothers and cousins. They hold up their own hands for inspection, and then they all grin at each other before digging back into their bread, swallowing the dirt along with the food.

'What are you lot smirking at?' their grandmother says. Amanda watches her raise the half-full glass of whiskey and drain it in one swallow. Her face looks almost purple in the light from the fire.

'Sit here by me,' she suddenly says to Amanda.

Amanda doesn't move.

'Come on here now.'

'Go on,' Seamus says.

Amanda squashes onto the rickety table bench where her grandmother sits with her eyes closed, breathing noisily. As Amanda stares, she opens her eyes and winks at Amanda.

'I had a babby like you,' she slurs, softly, into her ear, 'always fucking bawling.'

She looks straight at Amanda.

'Fucking ting, into the bog it went.'

Amanda puts her hand to her mouth and pokes out the bit of bread that is glued to the back of her tongue.

'Too many fucking childer altogether. Into the fucking bog with the childer.'

Amanda scrambles to her feet and goes to stand beside her mother. 'I want to go back to England,' she says, and gets hold of her mother's hand.

'So do I,' Barbara says, and gives her palm a squeeze. And they watch the proceedings together, Seamus talking about getting a bit of a land and everyone already calm again, like boiling kettles taken off the gas.

A bomb has gone off. She saw it on the teatime news; a mangled coach on the motorway, the back burnt black, ripped open and hanging off, seats almost touching the roadside. The news man tells them that those on board the coach were soldiers' families. The IRA did it, he says. Amanda saw an IRA caravan in Ireland. They'd gone to some little town somewhere for the day, eight of them packed into her aunty's little beetle car, she on her mum's knee, pressing right against the window. They were waiting at some traffic lights and she saw the caravan planted in the middle of a car park, plastered in posters, with the Irish flag with a gun on it fluttering on the top. One poster was huge and had a picture of men in balaclavas. Only their eyes were visible and they had guns in their hands. Above the men were the words *We have the answer!* Next to that was *Brits Out* with a torn Union Jack. The caravan door was open, and as they passed she saw a bearded man inside, sat thumbing through a pile of leaflets on a tiny table and she was suddenly worried about the way their English accents sounded. Her mum watched the news with her hands over her mouth, tears streaming down her face, and her dad sat there without saying a word, looking like he might smile at any minute.

And now Amanda hears people saying things whenever she is outside, angry, accusing voices that seem to belong to everyone; their next-door neighbours, people in shop queues, kids on bikes, grannies on buses, even teachers at school. 'Send the bloody lot back,' they say. 'Drop a few bombs over there, see how they like it' and 'Get the Army straight down to bloody Dublin'. It's been happening for months and months. When she goes into the shop with her brothers, a woman calls them savages. Mrs Dyer from the end house on the opposite side of the road is talking to someone in her garden as Amanda goes past.

'Hello,' Amanda says. Mrs Dyer carries on talking. Amanda thinks she hasn't heard her because she always says hello to her and she lets her help pick raspberries every summer.

'Hello,' she says again.

When Mrs Dyer turns, she is not smiling. She nods towards Amanda's house, and says to her friend, 'Goddamn Paddies. Worse than Pakis.'

'I'm not a bloody Paddy,' Amanda shouts, 'I was born here.'

They are having a party in the garden, making the most of the unlikely warm March. Seamus is away, settling his youngest sisters in, who have joined the rest of his siblings in Manchester where they will work as cleaners in the rich houses. Gran and Grandad are sat on kitchen chairs while Amanda and her brothers prepare to perform a show. Aunty Pammy strings the washing line between the fence and the shed and covers it with a blanket which Amanda, Tommo and Jamie crouch behind. Tommo whistles a tune and Jamie hums along. It is meant to sound like *Swan Lake*, which Aunty Pammy insisted on watching on BBC2 the night before. They draw back the blanket to reveal Amanda, with a net curtain wrapped around her waist. She goes up on her toes and then jumps to the side before putting her arms in the air and pirouetting. She flaps her hands like wings and then bends her knees and sinks to the floor. When she rises again, there is a single egg on the grass. Grandad is chuckling and Gran has to take her glasses off to wipe her eyes as the show comes to an end. Barbara laughs, a big, hearty laugh that seems to rise up from deep inside her, and then she dances around her children, humming a tune. Aunty Pammy claps in time. When Alan from next door comes out of his shed and looks away, bemused, Barbara doesn't bat an eye. The sun catches her clothes and bathes them in bold colour and she looks, Amanda thinks, like a woman from a magazine cover.

Seamus brings wind and grey rain back with him. His court summons, over Tommo, has finally arrived. Though Father Quinn has assured him he'll speak up for him when the day comes – will say he's a hard working man who deeply regrets what happened – Seamus is once again the dad Amanda recognises. He is back to cursing the fucking Brits and he yells and shouts although his fists remain in his pockets. Barbara has shrunk back into the gaps Seamus leaves as he moves around the house. Amanda hangs onto the edge of his inflating anger, waiting, like her brothers, for it to puncture. She keeps picturing the clifftop gulls she saw once, clinging to the rock face before being blasted off by the sudden force of the storm. Amanda and her brothers feel the need to end this uneasy stalemate and their Irish cousins have filled them with mutiny. They call him names, breathing them into each other's ears. They are always at it, on the stairs, in the garden, anytime he leaves a room.

'What are you bloody whispering about?'

'Nothing, Dad.'

'Shut it,' he says.

They know that they have their fingers on a button that detonates his fury until his temper is bursting at the seams. It is a button they can't resist from pressing and pressing. And they play tricks. They cut halfway through his bootlace so it snaps when he is getting ready for work. They poke a hole into his best jacket pocket with a knitting needle. And they goad him and congratulate each other on a job well done. Amanda has also found language to impress her brothers. She has new nicknames for their dad, 'Pope Seamus', 'Pontius Paddy' and 'Bogtrotter'. When he yelled at them for talking in the kitchen when he was trying to take a nap and made them go to bed in the middle of the afternoon, she called him 'Daddy Bagpuss'. This is Tommo's favourite.

When she left the front room door open, her dad said, 'Were you born in a fucking barn?'

'No, Dad, you must be thinking of Jesus,' she says, and takes a seat next to her brothers who are swallowing hard and making a noise like moths flapping against a light bulb.

Whenever he is out and they are in, especially the precious half hour when they are home from school and he is still at work, they make the most of it, rampaging around the house, jumping down the entire seven steps from stair landing to hall floor, chasing each other in and out of the kitchen and front room, spinning around the place making the foundations shake, ignoring their mother's pleas for calm. They let the dog lie by the fire, they leave a trail of contraband on the rug, crisp crumbs and sprinkles of chocolate and tiny sparks of sugar. They have jousting competitions with Dad's old newspapers, rolled up tight enough to deliver a blow. Jamie decides to be a dalek and gets the plunger stuck fast to his forehead. As the clock ticks off the minutes past 4pm – Dad's finishing time – she and Tommo place a foot on each shoulder as he lies on the ground and pull; it looks as if his skin will come off as it stretches further and further upwards. But the rubber seal gives in the end with a huge pop, and when Seamus gets in, the only sign of things being done in his absence is the large, angry red circle on Jamie's forehead. Seamus takes no notice of his kids, and sits himself down with his mug of tea and waits for his food.

Such fun sometimes goes, of course, too far in a game and it stops being play and becomes a war of sorts. One of Tommo's favourite games is pig herding. He chases them around the living room with Dad's cane, which he uses at first with mild violence but increasingly builds until he is raining blows down on them, and Amanda has to make a temporary alliance with Jamie and charge at Tommo with arms wheeling, landing punches until they manage to pull the stick off him. Or they play boxing or wrestling or IRA and turn on each other with the ferocity of Kilkenny cats, clawing and tearing at each other until blood drips and jaws ache and knuckles throb. Sometimes her brothers fight each other over which TV programme to watch, and after that Jamie ignores Tommo and plays with her. Most often she has to fight the two of them when they turn on her, ganging up and moving in to attack, holding her down and punching or pushing her over as she tries to walk out, tripping her up and then jumping on her as she falls. She learns, in the reality of her smaller body being of limited use against her older, stronger brothers, to use weapons. Knelt on and pummelled to give her a dead arm, she reaches for a fork and plunges it into Jamie's leg. Tommo, after not letting her join in their darts game, gets a dart in the back, then runs round in cartoon fashion, both hands reaching around his back, trying to get it out. And she throws things, so many things. When cornered, she will pick up the thing closest to hand and let it fly. Once she threw a small, thick whiskey glass at Tommo's head. There was a loud crack and blood seeped from a line across his temple. She was rooted to the spot as she watched him struggle to his feet and run to the door with hands cupped to catch the blood, more afraid that it would spill onto the carpet than of the wound itself.

But such in-fights are quickly forgotten when five o'clock looms. They circle their feeble wagons and watch their freedom evaporate. They rub out the trail of their happiness and sit and count the seconds until the back door opens and they have nothing, at this particular moment in time, to do to each other.

They are walking together to Mass with their granny and grandad and Aunty Pammy. Everyone has their best clothes on. Amanda has on a blue coat and white lace gloves and she holds Aunty Pammy's hand but lets go every now and again to stroke her fur coat. Her dad and grandad are talking quietly together at the back and her mum and gran are right behind her. Jamie and Tommo are quite a way in front, laughing about something. They are almost at the church, walking past Amanda's old school when they see three men from Dad's factory. Amanda knows one of them, his daughter is in the same year, and when she turned eleven Amanda was invited to the party. He moves to the side to let them past but the other two men, one fat, one skinny and very tall, stand there, blocking the path. The boys are too far ahead but the rest of them stop. Amanda searches for her Aunty Pammy's hand.

'Hello, Seamus,' the fat one says.

'How-ya,' Seamus said.

'Send a message home, eh, Seamus? Tell 'em to call off the dogs. That's a good lad.'

The two men laugh. The fat man makes a huh-huh-huh sound that stabs the air. Amanda pulls at her Aunty Pammy's arm.

'Why have we stopped?' she says.

'Hush up,' her granny says, and pulls Amanda to her side.

'Come on, Seamus,' her grandad says, 'let's get going now.'

Amanda's mum tries to move round the fat man but he steps sideways so she is trapped.

'Hope you're proud of your little half-breeds,' he says.

Her dad shoves past Aunty Pammy and her grandad and punches the fat man in the face. Amanda cries out as the man falls backwards onto the wall and slumps down, eyes closed, neck bent into the dent where part of the wall is missing. Tommo and Jamie have run back and are peering round each side of their grandad who is trying to stop them looking.

Her dad lifts his foot as if he will kick the man and then he changes his mind and kneels down, grabs his hair and starts banging the man's head against the stone. Amanda runs to him and tries to pull him away.

'No, Dad, no, Dad,' she says. Amanda starts shouting and crying at the same time, 'Stop it, stop it, stop it.'

Her grandad gets hold of her dad's other arm. 'God's sake. That's enough.'

Her dad stares wildly around him, as if blinded, before getting back to his feet. He shakes his head and looks at the other men, still stood there beside them.

'Seamus, I'm sorry,' the skinny man says. He puts his hand on Seamus' shoulder but Seamus shrugs him off.

'Get to fuck,' Seamus says to the fat man on the floor though he looks like he is asleep.

'Seamus, watch your language,' her granny says, and puts her arms around Amanda. Amanda feels her shaking through her coat. 'We'll be late for Mass.'

'Shove your bloody church,' Seamus says, and marches off in the direction of home. The skinny man is still saying sorry as Amanda's grandad herds everyone together and gets them moving.

When they get home, Seamus is in the front room with Graham and Bob, two of his hunting friends. They are all slightly drunk from Dad's homebrew, watching a western.

'Go out and play,' her mum says, handing them apples and biscuits. Amanda runs for the front door and out into the air. Her brothers head off in the direction of the hills, telling her she can't go with them. She goes instead down to the field opposite the house and finds the girls from her school and she joins them, plaiting grass stalks and inserting blue bells into the weave. She meets her brothers on the way in when they are called for tea. Seamus and his friends take their plates and go back to the TV and Amanda and her brothers take advantage of their father's absence at the table to poke each other with their forks, ignoring their mum's hissed commands to stop. When they finish their food, they hover in the kitchen until their mum goes into the front room, then they follow her and sit in a cramped pile at one end of the sofa. Amanda watches in dismay as her mother picks up plates and leaves again, she knows she will sit in the kitchen with a pile of magazines and newspapers.

'What's the film?' Tommo asks his dad. Bob, with the big, black moles on his face, starts to answer. His words collide in mid-air with Seamus' voice.

'Keep it shut.'

Bob stops speaking as if he were the one being spoken to. Amanda sits with her brothers in a line, brooding and bored. Tommo pinches her and she cries out and gets a warning look from Seamus. Jamie is on the end of the sofa, parallel to Dad's chair and just out of his sightline, and he sits pulling faces at her and Tommo, slowly moving his hands to his ears to pull out each lobe sideways, eyes crossed, lips pursed. Then he makes an angry face and mimes shouting and puffs out his cheeks. Dad sees the movement out of the corner of his eye and spins round in his chair, but Jamie's face is already neutral again. Amanda can feel her brothers watching her, daring her to do something. She picks up the *Radio Times* and points in exaggerated fashion to the cover photo. It is Les Dawson, dressed as a woman and pulling a silly face. Amanda turns her finger so that it points towards Seamus, and says, 'What a big ugly pig.' Her brothers titter beside her and she rattles the TV guide as loud as she dares before placing it back on her knee. She raises her finger once again towards her dad, and says, 'What a thick, horrible man.'

'Proper little entertainer, aren't you?' Seamus says, and his laugh sounds like a dog barking. Amanda feels her brothers stiffen next to her and she can't think of anything to say.

'Get up,' he says.

'Why?'

'Come on, get up,' he says, still smiling. Amanda stands up but doesn't move.

'Stand there,' he says, and nods his head towards the unlit fire. She stands near the TV side of the hearth, out of range of his boots. He flicks his fingers to the right and she shuffles over.

'Sing something,' he says.

'What?' Amanda is confused.

'Sing us something. Come on, entertain us.' He looks round

at his friends and then he smiles at his sons and then he looks back at her and laughs loudly.

'C'mon, sing something.'

'I don't want to.'

'Sing us a bloody song.'

'I don't want to. Please, Dad. I don't want to.'

'You're not sitting back down until you fucking sing.'

Amanda sings the first song that comes into her head, the one her mother used to sing, when she still baked.

'Killing me softly…' she sings but can't remember the next line, confuses it with the chorus and sings words that don't fit the rhythm. Her voice falters and goes much too high as she hunts for the tune. Seamus begins to clap along and she glances up and sees him watching and grinning and her brothers staring and Bob just looking at his knees. Graham is laughing along with her father, and she feels the heat in her face and the line of sweat that tickles just under her fringe. She starts to cry and Bob jumps up and strides to the door.

'Seamus, I need to go now,' he says.

'You'll miss the end of the film,' Seamus says.

'I've seen it a hundred times,' he says, and is out the door. Graham follows him so Seamus gets up and goes to see his friends off. Amanda stands there with tears falling, not knowing if she should move. She can taste the beery air now; it sticks in the back of her throat like the time she got a mouthful of her aunty's hairspray. She hears her dad come back in but doesn't look up.

'Sit the fuck down,' he says. Amanda walks to the sofa and sits down. She doesn't know who it is that puts out a hand to sit softly on top of her arm, because her eyes are tightly closed. She pulls away, curls her arms against her chest.

The film ends and the news comes on and they watch the pictures again; that same shot of a twisted metal skeleton once full of people like them, that are now fragments of flesh and bone blasted across the concrete.

'Fucking Brits,' her dad says.

They have just started their chippy supper when the sound of Seamus, singing outside, sails in through the window. They sit, forks raised, listening. Barbara sets her plate down on the rug and goes to the kitchen, and Amanda and the boys follow her. The kitchen door is open and several voices are talking outside, giving instructions to each other. Through the voices, the sound of Seamus, his words blurring together as if bubbling up from underwater. Amanda waits until her mother has gone outside and then she goes to the window.

'Jesus Christ,' she says, and Jamie and Tommo jostle with her to take a look. Seamus is flanked by the Jackson brothers, Peter and Paul, who go ferreting with Seamus. The two little dicky birds Amanda calls them to her brothers. They wobble around as they try to hold him up. All of them are drunk. Their dad sweeps them this way and that as he tries to get to the back door. When he sees his family watching, he holds his arms up to the sky and shouts.

'That judge can go fuck himself.'

'Seamus, come in,' Barbara hisses, looking towards the neighbours' houses opposite.

Seamus isn't listening, just laughing. 'I fucking won it, lads. Didn't I win it?'

'You did, Seamus. Now get yourself inside.'

'No fucking English cunt will tell an Irishman what to do,' he says, and Seamus starts dancing along the path and then back down again.

'I fucking won it, boys.'

148

He weaves up the path then misses his footing, staggers into the rockery, trampling the pansies and sweet peas that Barbara planted. He falls against the lattice fence, which gives way under him, and he falls backwards into the garden. Even as his head rebounds off the grass he is snoring loudly. Amanda giggles, watching him asleep in the garden. Jamie and Tommo don't join in and her solitary laughing sounds small inside the long kitchen so she stops. Seamus' friends eventually manage to get him upright and he stumbles over to the jungle part of the garden, unzips his trousers and pisses against the hedge. They stand, helpless, until he is finished, and then bring him inside. They are sweating from the effort of keeping him upright and sit him at the table. Seamus pulls his wallet out of his pocket and scrabbles for a tatty piece of newspaper balled inside it. He unfolds the clipping and smooths it out on the table. Amanda sneaks a look at it from behind him. There is a picture of a baby laughing. The way the paper is creased she can only read the first line: *Murdered by own father.*

'The fucking bastard,' Seamus says, 'look at what he did. They should fucking hang him for it.' He starts to cry. His tears drip onto the table.

'What a piece of shit,' he says.

Amanda looks at her brothers but they are already walking back into the front room. She watches her dad weeping for a child he doesn't know, and then Barbara goes over and snatches the bit of paper.

'For God's sake. Get him to bed,' she says.

The men make their way slowly up the stairs, crashing and banging, one in front of Seamus and one behind, and Amanda thinks of Laurel and Hardy trying to move the piano up a hill. When they move out of sight, the sound of slipping and tripping, accompanied by muffled swearing, continues. Eventually Seamus' friends reappear.

'He's settled now, Barbara,' Paul tells her, as if Seamus were a baby.

When Barbara doesn't answer, Paul looks at his brother, and says, 'Right then, we'll be off.'

Barbara closes the door behind them and they go back into the front room and start again on their food. Amanda watches her mother try a chip, then put it back down before throwing the plate against the wall where the fish explodes and sprays white and yellow scraps everywhere. Amanda feels it hit her hair at the back and she looks round to see peas and chips sliding down the wall and over the sideboard.

'Eat your food,' Barbara says, and moves over to the corner where she starts to clean up the mess. Amanda and Tommo wolf theirs down and when Jamie puts his, unfinished, on the floor, they lurch towards it, both of them getting their hands on it at the same time. They have a silent tug of war as their mother picks the greasy bits off the carpet, stacking them on one half of her broken plate. Amanda is too busy to notice the good times sliding out the door.

The next morning, Seamus is back in his suit. Amanda and her brothers are assembled in the front room with their mum. He takes his wallet from the sideboard drawer and puts it into his trouser pocket. He picks up his suitcase.

'Where are you going?' Amanda asks.

'Away from the fucking Brits,' he says, though he doesn't look at her, only at her mother.

'I'll come back for you when I've found a place to stop. We can make a better go of it over there. And we can build a house, bigger than this one.'

'Right, Dad.'

'Behave yourselves for yer mother.'

'Yes, Dad.'

'Give my regards to the McGinnises.' Barbara says.

'I should be back in a week or so.'

They stand at the door, waving as the taxi ferries Seamus round the corner and up the hill and away. Amanda starts to dance around the hallway and then grabs at Jamie and

Tommo and has them jumping up and down. She yells into the ceiling, 'Yeah, yeah, yeah.' The slap across her face stops her in her tracks.

'He's still your bloody father.'

Amanda raises her fist to her mother's face and holds it there. Barbara doesn't try to turn away from it. She just looks at it while her face closes down as if the fist were a key in a prison door. Tommo steps up next to Amanda and covers her fist with his hand and Jamie puts his arms across her though she makes no attempt to move across the tiny scrap of space between them. Amanda looks at her mother and she can see at that very second all the possible things that this action means, all the possible futures ahead of her and she doesn't know what do so she laughs, but it comes out like a sob.

Amanda watches her brothers dragging the huge bag down the stairs between them. They stand at the door, smiling thinly at her in between pushing their mother's hands off them as she tries to pull them back inside.

She realised then what their push for part-time jobs had been for, the paper rounds and the lawn mowing and the weekend shifts cleaning spuds in the chip shop. She'd known about their secret stash of money. Amanda puts herself between them and the door as she watches her mother paw at Tommo's and Jamie's denim-clad arms, struggling to get purchase on the slippery fabric.

'You're being stupid.'

'Don't start, Mum,' Tommo says.

'You've got to finish school. You've only a few months left.'

'We'll be in touch when we've found somewhere in Manchester.'

'Please don't do this. At least wait for your father to come back.'

'Not on your life,' Tommo said.

'Don't cry, Amanda,' Jamie says, and bends down and gives her a hug that is loose and awkward and she tries to hug him back but he's already finished and they end up holding each other's shoulders like two wrestlers readying to grapple. Tommo nods at Jamie who grabs a single handle.

'At least wait for your dad to come back. So he can talk to you, love.'

'Not a fucking chance.' Tommo pushes his mother's hands away.

'Don't you dare bloody swear at me. Go then. See how far a pair of bloody kids can get. He'll have the police onto you.' She walks into the front room and slams the door.

'Let's go,' he says to Jamie and he puts his hands on Amanda's shoulders. Though she tries to make herself solid and heavy he moves her easily from the door, and then leaves. Amanda follows them down the path and out the gate and around the corner, calling their names over and over.

'Let me come.'

'For fuck's sake, go back in,' Tommo shouts and he turns round and makes swiping motions with his free hand before wiping it across his eyes. Jamie keeps his back turned, his shoulders heaving.

'Don't leave me,' she yells at their backs as they wobble up the hill with the bulging bag. The rest of her words are clogged in her throat, like milk drunk in the middle of summer and she watches, tears and snot dripping into her mouth, until they disappear over the top of the road. Then she goes back to the house and into her room where she lies with her head under her pillow.

Amanda is watching cartoons when Seamus returns. He bursts into the house, mid-morning, whistling and singing and, for a second, Amanda thinks her brothers are back. She is half out of her seat before she hears him asking where everyone is, and the tiny hope crashes and she sits back down as he strides in. In his excitement he starts talking, in the absence of the others, to her, speaking so quickly that the words get jammed in his mouth, one word half swallowed by the one following, his sentences unfinished before another one starts. Amanda sits watching him jabber on as his pulls at the suitcase straps and throws open the case until her mother walks in and finally gets a word in edgeways, tells him that he no longer has sons.

'They've gone,' she says, with words as slow as his were fast.

'Who've gone?'

'Jamie. Tommo. They've gone. They packed their bags and they went.' Tears fall into the purple dints under her eyes.

His smile fades as the realisation seeps in. 'How the fuck could you let this happen?'

Her mum says nothing, just stands there, one hand holding her neck, the other round her waist. When Seamus turns his gaze towards her, Amanda shrinks down in the sofa, pushes back so hard the edge of the wooden strut stabs into her back.

'Get the fuck out,' he says.

Amanda runs, going the long way to the door, past her mum. As she races upstairs, she hears him yelling, hears things thrown around, the slap of a hand against skin and the front door yanked open and footsteps down the path. She climbs into bed and closes her eyes and her brothers immediately appear, sharing that bag, sharing a new life and Amanda sees, suddenly, how big they are, how they towered above her at the door. She hears *Let's go* over and over, two tiny words that meant something so very big, that meant that they were gone, just like that.

When she wakes, she listens for sounds of her mother, but all she can hear is Seamus crashing and banging around. She stays in her room for hours and still her mother doesn't appear. When she hears Seamus coming upstairs, she hurries to the wardrobe, opens the door and crawls inside where she sits as still as possible. When Seamus comes in, she can hear him moving around and it goes dark every time he walks past the slice of light coming through the crack in the door. Her breathing is loud in the squashed space. When Seamus stops moving, she holds her breath until her ears start to whistle, she is afraid the sound will blast out of her and through the door. When she finally gives way, air wheezing out of her nostrils, she still can't hear him and she thinks he might be laying in wait until she comes out from hiding. She stays in there all afternoon, watching the dust dance in the chink of light, cramp twisting her calf muscles and hunger bending her in half. She emerges when her mother finally calls up to see if she is home, her legs crumpling slightly as she heads down for food.

'Get fucking out of it.' Seamus says, as she opens the kitchen door.

Amanda thinks he means her again until she sees Bonnie's head retracting from around the back door. Amanda is surprised to see her father stood at the cooker, thumping one pan down and picking another up and swirling it around so that something sloshes quietly inside. Amanda joins her mother at the table and tries to rub away the pins and needles in her legs. Seamus gets butter from the fridge and slams the door causing the fridge to rock back and forth. It makes the very same tick-tock sound as the front room clock. He has made a hodgepodge of food, like breakfast and supper and tea all in one. Bacon and boiled eggs and fish fingers are all thrown together on one plate and three bowls of tomato soup sit next to a golden grain loaf and some lumps of Lancashire cheese. They have all sat at their usual places, which leaves a big empty space at one side of the table. Seamus shakes his head constantly as he butters his bread.

'How could you fucking lose them?' he says, as if her brothers are a pair of gloves that her mum has misplaced.

School feels more and more like being in a cage that is too small for all the kids packed inside it. She is surrounded by jostling limbs and raucous squawking at unfunny jokes and stupid gossip. There is a clique of girls who wouldn't say boo to a goose on their own, but who have formed a sly band that call her names behind her back. She wanders, here and there, to hear the final syllables from mouths that clamp shut when they see her. The teachers have to monitor her constantly, because she is a now a 'runner', given half a chance. She knows that nearly all the teachers dislike her for this, for adding extra duties to their already long list of responsibilities. There are two types of teacher who dislike her: those, like Mr Adams, who hide nothing, who openly sneer and chivvy whenever she is in their sights, and those who think they hide it behind their over-bright voices and pantomime smiles. They smile as they spy on her from one end of the school to the other. They smile as they badger her to get a move on as she idles along corridors towards the classrooms. They smile as they tell her to take off the denim jacket that she holds closed across her chest to disguise her breasts that she knows are deformed because her dad once teased her about them in front of her brothers. She knows they are bigger than normal girls' breasts, so much so that her blouse buttons strain, and when she has to take off her jacket she holds it high up against her chest and she waits until the smiling teachers have moved off and puts it straight back on again. They smile as they guard the main school gates and check where she is heading to. Three teachers have huge smiles that stretch so far across their faces the whole day long that she imagines them taking them off when they get home, sitting blank-faced on the sofa as they rub their aching cheeks.

There is only Mr K in her corner. His full name is Barnat Kramm but the kids call him Mr K, except for the retards who call him Mr Kraut or Barnat the Boche because they're too thick to get that he's not German. Mr K, for some reason, likes her. He jokes with her whenever he sees her, asking if she has any fags on her or saying what a nice day it is when the rain is pouring. He looks out for her too. He once caught Adams yelling at her for not wearing her tie, shouting at her as if she'd just set fire to someone.

'I think she's heard enough now. You can see she's upset.'

'Have it your way,' he said, and walked away laughing.

Mr K knows how she likes to learn, his English classes are still her favourite. He throws ideas at her and expects her to throw her own back. He makes her work. When they have to give talks to the class, he always makes her go first. When she reads aloud, she gets caught up in the book. She

156

leaps outside of herself and into the story and she is telling everyone, as she reads with her voice rising and falling, what she is seeing. She is letting them know when to be surprised and when to be sad, trying to lead them through the book instead of sitting there staring out the window or poking each other with their pens. Sometimes they start laughing and Mr K walks to them and smacks his hand down on top of their desk and the bang of it swallows up all their chat. They've just finished reading *Animal Farm* and Mr K asked them what they thought about the book.

'I think the pigs are wrong,' she'd said, 'they shouldn't have become corrupt and all capitalist, like Thatcher, sir. Communism could make us all equal but they turned their back on it.'

The rest of the class make yawning noises.

'Do you think equality made my parents flee, Amanda? Do you think that's what's happening in North Korea or East Germany or Tibet?'

'I don't understand, sir.'

'No, and you won't, not for years. But it's good that you think about these things.'

When the class is over, he tells her to stay behind. He hands her a pile of marked homework and some books.

'Your stories are excellent. And I think you might like these,' he says, and points to the top one. It has a picture of a boy in a white robe, holding a gold cup. She reads the title *The Golden Goblet* though she is having to look at the book the wrong way round.

'Don't get all sulky at me for this one, it looks like a kid's book but I think it's bloody brilliant and it will do you good to read it.'

She is dumbstruck by him swearing so she just nods and picks up the pile.

'I saw your arm this morning.'

Her fingers fly to her sleeves, making sure they're down past the wrists, as far as they will go.

'Who did this?'

She doesn't answer at all, pulls at a button on her cardigan.

'You know you can talk to me, don't you?'

'Yes, sir.'

'I will do my very best to help you. I can promise you that.'

'Yes, sir, thanks.'

'It doesn't have to be today, it can be any time.'

The button flies across the room with a sharp crack as its cotton chains snap. They watch the button fly for a few yards, then hit the table where it bounces and spins, right on the edge. It slows down, as if it is going to settle there, but it is too far gone and it goes over, hits the carpet and stops dead. It makes no more noise.

'We'll leave it there, okay?'

'Yes sir, thanks.'

She takes a few steps.

'Wait a second,' he says.

Her shoulders drop ever so slightly, the door creaks, uncertainly. He comes over and stretches out his hand.

'I forgot I had something else for you. It's a tape, the singers I was telling you about.'

She looks at the little black cassette in his hand and takes it, quickly, trying not to touch his fingers.

'Thanks, sir.'

She is almost outside the school when she realises she has left her bag on the chair. When she goes back to the room, she doesn't knock, thinking he'll be gone. He is still by his desk, crying into a hanky with flowers along the edge. Miss King, who everyone says is his girlfriend, is sitting on the edge of the desk, swinging her legs to and fro, talking to him,

'... than most people would do. You can't help everyone, and she's pretty far gone.'

Amanda backs out of the room without them seeing her. His girlfriend is right, she thinks, she knows exactly what she is. Every fucking day, when she has to walk through those gates she feels as though she's struggling to stay afloat. She's being swept away and Mr K, on his own, is not enough.

The suits are back, stood in the kitchen with Barbara. Amanda has been out with Aunty Pammy and her gran, and stops in the doorway when she sees the suits looking at her, hoping that they've brought Jamie and Tommo back.

'How are you, Amanda?' the man asks her. They always know her name. She doesn't know them from Adam, yet they always greet her cheerily, first-name terms, like they're her friend. She doesn't say anything at all, just bites her fingers and looks at them. When Seamus comes in, he takes one look and points to outside.

'Get out of my fucking house, now.'

'Now, Mr Duffy, you need to calm down.'

'You'll either leave now or I'll throw you out. You can get to fuck.'

'We're only here…'

Seamus isn't listening. He flings open the back door and moves right up close to the man.

'Now,' he says.

The man shuffles past him and the woman trots behind.

Minutes later, Amanda hears something creaking in the back garden. She peeps out of the window and sees her dad breaking things and throwing them on a fire. She can see their dart board, bent in half with the metal rim hovering above the numbers, the teddy she's had as long as she can remember sat in the middle like an accused medieval witch. He's just thrown a small pile of dry old comics onto the fire, which has the flames roaring. And now he breaks Jamie's little theatre that he made years ago, spending months on it. He'd cut out old bits of wood and hammered them together and then painted it with the leftover tin of white paint he'd found in the shed. He'd taken lights from his calculators and put them along the roof and they lit up in a line of red when you flicked a switch. She'd sat all evening with her brothers once, cutting out and colouring little paper figures and then sliding them up and down the grooves Jamie had gouged into the wood along the stage floor. Seamus brings his boot down on the top of it, which smashes the thin wood to bits, and then he feeds it into the fire. The figures are still stuck in place and when they catch fire, tiny pieces of ash blast up into the air like little grey fireworks.

Seamus has sent messages, through every Irish family he knows, to Manchester, London, Liverpool, even Glasgow, and he's waiting for his boys to be delivered back to him before he goes back to Ireland. In the meantime, he's taken over the household and runs it like an army camp, organising the house from top to bottom, clearing everything out ready for moving. Barbara sits, staring into space, but Seamus is never still; he is always dragging something from its hiding place and destroying it. Old blankets and clothes are thrown into tatty cardboard boxes for the bin men to take away. The clutter from the cistern and the cupboard under the stairs is gone. The whole place is cleaner than it has ever been. Amanda is sent to dust every bit of furniture in the place. When she reaches the front room, she starts on the TV and her mum doesn't complain even though she is deliberately blocking her view. Barbara no longer cooks, nor eats at the table anymore, saying that she has lost her appetite, though Amanda has found her, whenever Seamus has fallen asleep in his chair, sneaking food from the cupboards and fridge. Amanda has to sit with him, every teatime, when he wears his fury like a thick coat. If she makes even a slight eating noise he bangs his knife down and calls her a little animal. She now eats tiny amounts of food at a time and sips at her water, trying to swallow soundlessly as she listens to him chew and slurp at his tea. She nips at her food, be it Seamus' chips that slide down easily or his gristly stew that she has to dislodge from her throat with water. The smell of tonight's tea hits her as soon as she opens the door, a sickly, sweet smell from the frying sausages. When the sausages are put in front of her, her stomach flips. She cuts a tiny piece off one of them and holds it to her nose, looking at the funny blue-white speckling that runs through the middle.

'I think it's off, Dad,' she says.

'Shut it,' he says.

'It smells funny.'

'It's fucking fine. Get it ate.'

Seamus takes a bite of his and swallows it, then puts his fork down and takes a long swig of his tea. He eats the chips and beans and then takes the plate and scrapes the sausages into the bin.

'Get that lot finished,' he says, and pushes the bolt firm into its lock and takes his tea into the front room.

Amanda sits there for a while and then slips off her shoes and gets up and crosses the kitchen in her socks. She moves the bolt fraction by fraction so that it doesn't do its metal shrieking. She thinks of all the times that she helped her brothers like this. Whenever Barbara had burned the burgers or boiled the beans, or dropped some grey-looking meat onto their plates, they would move it around, putting the tiniest forkfuls to their mouths whenever Seamus looked at them. Once he had gone into the front room, Tommo and Jamie would leave it to Amanda to work the bolt free as they listened out for him and she'd throw her food over the hedge into the jungle bit of the garden. She'd do the same for them, one lot of slop after another arcing over the hedge, and then she'd ease the bolt closed again and take her seat. And they'd wait a while and then tell Dad they'd finished and he'd come in to inspect their plates and the bin. Sometimes their bravery knew no bounds and at bedtime they'd steal biscuits from the cupboard and she would sit in bed in the dark munching. She would feel the crumbs later, rolling under her back and bum as she fell asleep.

Seamus has opened the kitchen door open as silently as Amanda slides the bolt. He sees her at the back door.

'Sit fucking down and eat yer tea.'

Amanda almost drops her plate and struggles to keep it steady as she makes her way back to the table, watching the sausages slide around in their own grease. Seamus sits opposite her, watching her until she puts the first pink, stinking, piece into her mouth. She swallows without chewing. She only manages to do this twice more, about a half-sausage's worth, before her stomach starts hurting. The kitchen door opening makes them both jump and by the time Barbara is at the kettle with her mug, Amanda is already on her knees on the floor by the dog. Pieces of sausage come straight back up. Bonnie runs up and sniffs at the little pieces of meat and then wrinkles her nose and goes back to her corner. Barbara lets her cup drop onto the worktop where it rattles around and runs over to Amanda.

'For Christ's sake, Seamus, what have you done to her?'

Barbara asks her if she's okay, and Amanda is so glad to see her that she grins broadly even as her stomach turns hard as concrete.

The weather has turned icy overnight but it does nothing to dampen the heat of Seamus' rage. Amanda can almost see it; it is because she is not one of his sons. And even if she was a son, she's going to get it now anyway because Tommo and Jamie are free and clear and there is no one to share the burden anymore. In the evening they sit in the front room by the blazing fire. If Barbara says anything, Seamus shushes her and she sighs and tuts and goes back to her magazines. Amanda tries to whisper to her mum, and he snarls at her to shut the fuck up.

The next day is the first day of half term and Amanda is up early in the morning, before Seamus wakes up and gives her something to do. She runs up the hill and sits on the grass behind her friend's house, waiting for her to wake up. She stays out until four o'clock and goes home when Barbara shouts for her, her stomach knotting with hunger. After tea she asks if she can go back out, but Seamus says no, so she has to sit in the front room and when Barbara gets up and doesn't come back, Amanda is alone with him, in the silence that chokes, where all she can hear is his faint snorting like a faraway bull. Her throat does that funny internal burping it always does when she swallows too much and when Seamus moves, she holds her breath until her ribs ache as she waits to see if he has heard it. She is desperate for a pee but daren't ask so she holds it in for hours and when finally Seamus tells her to go to bed, she can't move because of the feeling of fluid threatening to flood.

'Shift yourself,' he says, and she jumps up and walks in a crab-like way, inching up the stairs. When she reaches the toilet, she doesn't have time to undress but sits down and pisses through her jeans. She wipes the toilet seat clean afterwards and then changes into dry clothes. She finds an old plastic bag, and rolls her pants into a sodden ball and places them inside. When she goes to bed, she expects to lie awake, as she always does but instead she sleeps – deeply – and without dreams.

By the time she gets up, Barbara has already gone into Rochdale. Amanda knows that she will be out the best part of the day, coming home on the last bus. Seamus is roaring at her to get out of bed so she gets dressed and goes downstairs where she watches him get her cereal ready. After breakfast she once again has to sit with him as he sits in his chair, watching the football. She pinches her nose so that she doesn't sneeze. Whenever Seamus moves, she shrinks down.

'Pick the bits up off the carpet,' he says, not looking at her.

She gets down on her hands and knees and is glad of the movement as she crawls around the front room, pinching at bits of fluff, grains of dirt, miscellaneous specks, collecting them in a balled fist. She's learned to inch her way behind the sofa where, shielded from view, she pulls faces at him through the furniture.

'Get yer fucking self round here.'

She moves then to the carpet by the TV.

'Get these bits here,' and points to the rug under his feet.

She crawls slowly to his chair, taking as much time as she dares.

'Come on, yer fucking slowcoach.'

He kicks at her once, upends her onto her side, and then sits looking at her as she looks up at him and he suddenly looks tired. He motions with his hand to the air above his head and so she gets up off the floor and runs up the stairs and sits in her room.

In the evening she hears Barbara come home and a few minutes later she comes into Amanda's bedroom with a cheese sandwich and some digestives. After handing them to her, she goes into her own bedroom. Amanda bolts them down and then drinks from the bathroom tap. As she returns to her room she hears Seamus' friends arrives and the click of beer bottles against the table. Amanda lies on her bed and starts to re-read the book Mr K gave her. It's about an Egyptian boy who wants to be a goldsmith, but whose life is ruled by his evil step-brother, who starves and beats him. The book is far too young for her but she reads it all the time because the boy escapes in the end, and even before this he has adventures with papyrus collectors and reed cutters and tomb robbers, and he eats food that she's never had: flat breads with honey, dates and dried fish which she thinks sounds disgusting, and water that he spoons from a stone trough in the yard. The boy wears an amulet to ward off bad luck and she feels like the book is her own amulet, like this boy is her friend, as if he exists when she reads about him and watches over her. She keeps the book under her pillow so that even if it's too dark to read, she can feel it under her cheek. She eats up the simple words, getting through chapters in minutes, and she's almost at the end of the book when she hears Seamus and his friends pissing in the garden, which they do every time they drink. Barbara used to fight with him about it, said she was ashamed to look anyone in the eye when they did such things, but she doesn't challenge him anymore. They are making even more noise than usual tonight. Amanda opens the window to listen. They are laughing raucously and joking about something or other.

'I'm finished with this shite-hole of a country. Fucking Englishman's law. It don't sit well with an Irishman.'

'Aye, Seamus. It's not my fucking law either, it's the fucking rich English.'

The pissing finishes and they are quiet for a while. Then her dad speaks again.

'I should have my fucking lads with me. Instead I have her, that little fat useless ting who won't even eat a bit of meat without fucking bawling.'

They go back into the house. Amanda walks to the mirror and sees those awful, bright blue eyes, just like his. 'You're fatter than me, you fat fucking pig!' she shouts through the floor. When she looks at her reflection again, she sees her eyes shrinking and her face expanding. Her eyes are like two tiny lamps in the middle of her fat, white face. She goes back to bed and starts to read again. Nothing happens. She is not leaving her body the way she usually does, it's as if she is glued to the mattress. The book can't save her or stop her being what she is. She can't live inside it. She's here and there is no point to anything. She rips the book in half and throws it across the room.

Amanda vaguely recognises the girl from church, she's another of the half-Irish. She has dark hair almost the same colour as hers, though her eyes are the grey blue, not sky blue kind. She is freckled and friendly and her pretty face is smiling as she walks over.

'Hi.'

'Hi.'

'Is your dad Seamus Duffy?

'Why?'

'Aw, he's lovely, your dad is. When he does his football rounds, he always brings us soccer cards. And he's always acting daft, tickling my little sister and pretending to box with me.'

Amanda tries not to let this information in. She's always felt a secret strength through her thoughts, that no matter how much shit Seamus shoves through the letterbox of her mind, leaving it to stink and fester there in the entryway, the door is locked to him. She knows he hates it every time he catches her lost in her thoughts, shouting at her, asking what the hell she's gawping at. But now that door has been battered down and he's stormed inside her head and is smashing the bit of her she keeps hidden inside.

'When?'

'What?'

'When did he do it?'

'He does it all time. He's great, is Seamus. You're lucky.'

The girl is still smiling and she wants to knock her teeth in, wants to punch her and punch her until she can't smile any fucking more. She pushes past her and runs down the corridor, straight past Mr K.

'Slow down, Amanda.'

'Go fuck yourself.'

She keeps on running, aiming for the stairs that lead down to the south exit. When she reaches the door, she realises that she has nowhere to run to, so she sits on the floor. By the time Mr K catches up to her, she is beating her fists against her head, tears streaming, and he sits down beside her and hugs her. She struggles at first but then she just sits by him, like a broken doll. Eventually he takes her to the nurse's office where she sits on a trolley with a glass of water. Mr K pats her shoulder for a while and then goes off to his next class, leaving a draft of cool air where he stood.

Seamus starts on her as soon as she gets through the door.

'Where the fuck have you been?'

She sees the spittle fly from his mouth and thinks of his foot on her back and his fist in her eye, thinks of him using soft words to that girl and her friends.

'Here and there.'

'What did you fucking say?'

'I said *here* and *there*.'

'I'll fucking swing for you in a minute.'

'I don't give a flying fuck.'

He comes stomping over and makes a grab for her, but she ducks and steps backwards. She is burning.

'I know about you giving cards to that girl. You fucking hypocrite,' she says.

He stares at her for a long time, his mouth open as if she were levitating right there above the tiles.

'Your tea's ready.'

'I don't want it.'

'You'd better want it.'

'I don't want anything you've made. Give it to her.'

'Shut the fuck up.'

She looks right in his face and then walks over to the window. She hits it hard, with the side of her fist. The glass booms and breaks and splinters cover her hair like confetti.

'Bogtrotter,' she says.

The first punch knocks her into the wall and the blows come in thick and fast. Then he picks her up and swings her, like a battering ram, before he lets her go. She flies for a second before she hits the floor. She jumps back to her feet and screams,

'You're nothing but a fucking bogtrotter.' She walks away from him into the hall.

When his boot connects with the back of her knees, her head snaps back and all her limbs give way at once. She is not afraid anymore, she doesn't even care that her mum doesn't appear, doesn't shout for her, she no longer hopes she will run in. She tries to open her eyes but her vision blurs so much she has to close them again. She is drifting away from the grunting her dad makes as he keeps stamping, and although she hears and feels things in her body crunch, nothing hurts at all. She is rising upwards, carried along inside this soft bubble where she is free. She watches herself, curled up on the carpet. And then it all stops. All she can hear is the sound of her own breath, a tiny panting as if she were a dog in a hot car. She begins to move and then sees that her father is still there. He is watching her as she squirms on the floor.

'Have you had enough?' he says.

She looks at her hand that caught the top of a nail that sticks up from the cracked kitchen tile. It is dripping blood from a crescent-shaped cut. She looks back at him, at the froth bubbling on his bottom lip, and she knows that this is all he is now, this is all he can do.

'Kill me if you want. I'll fucking die hating you.'

He raises his boot again and she can see a grass stem ground deep into the rubber sole, before the boot blocks out her vision. The boot hovers then retracts. He walks out of the room.

'At last,' she says, and laughs, so fast and hard it's like a machine gun firing at his back.

Part Seven
The Aftermath

Her new shrink smiles a lot less than the other one but his lips are dry and he is beardless. He is bigger than the other shrink, huge, in fact. Not as bulky as her dad, but much taller. When she sits in her chair and watches him walk around his desk, it seems as if he has inflated himself like the hulk and is almost touching the ceiling. His black hair comes to a peak at the front and he shapes his foreign sounds with pointy incisors that cut and clip each word. He is like the vampires in the late-night horror films she watches when she should be in bed. He often tells her it is a great thing that she keeps feeding her intellect because she is very bright, but that it is not her job to worry about the entire world. He moves around the room as he speaks, and when he gets out of her line of vision the hairs on the back of her neck stand up and her mind repeats the word 'feeding' and she thinks of his spiky teeth coming for her jugular. Her body is a hard knot until the hour is up. She will ache for days after the session as if they'd been running for an hour together instead of diving into her mind.

'How are things at school?' He seems to chew the words with his fangs so that they sound slightly mauled.

'Okay.'

Amanda started back at school in the September and she tried her very best to stay put. She feels as if her mind has come loose inside her head, like it's a coin tossed into one of those spiral charity boxes, with all her thoughts and feelings and memories spinning and corkscrewing until they land, tangled together somewhere dark and fuzzy and unclear. She battles with her body, which doesn't want to sit still. Her stomach churns and gurgles, her boots drum softly against the legs of her chair, some of her fingers doodle in margins while the others are inserted one at a time into her mouth where she bites all her nails and then the skin around the her nails, nipping and ripping until blood trickles from torn wicks. She is slipping underneath the lessons. The words spoken by teachers, that she used to know, clog up her brain in undigested lumps. She used to read things in textbooks, just the once, and have their meanings chained together in her mind but information is now unlinked strings of words. Her mind is, instead, full of the shit that people say to her all day long. She hears the whispers all around her. Every breath taken in a classroom or a corridor is like swallowing stones. When teachers close the doors of classrooms they clang shut like prison gates. Her heart races and sweat trickles.

'How are things at home?'
    'Okay.'
Her dad has been gone almost a year now and the intoxicating promise of all that freedom has turned into something sour and bitter. For months she was overcome with all the choices she had and often ended up sitting completely still on her bed, butterflies inside her just with knowing that she can move whenever she wants. At first she enjoyed listening to this new kind of silence. She could go in and out of the front room and up and down the stairs and nothing at all was yelled. One day, she opened all the windows, running from room to room and rattling the half-rusted handles from side to side until she prised them off their stubby latches. She started reading books in the front room while Barbara read her magazines. It felt like something magical was about to happen. It felt, she realised, exactly like those few Christmases they'd had at Gran's, when everyone was squashed around the small table in the kitchen. Nobody noticed that she passed her meat to Tommo and Jamie and

they could chat as much as they wanted. After dinner, Dad would sit talking with Grandad and Aunty Pammy and Mum would hum along to Abba records and Gran played board games with them and told them to help themselves to sweets out of a big round tin.

And she thinks about them, the last time they were all together, at New Year's Eve, to see in the new decade. They did the conga, on the very first stroke of midnight, even Gran and Grandad joining in, snaking out the door with Aunty Pammy shrieking and tickling Amanda's waist. They laughed and danced their way down the garden and out the gate where Aunty Pammy pushed Amanda to the front to lead the troop. It was only when they came back that Amanda saw her dad glaring through the window.

Aunty Pammy cajoled Barbara into getting a job in the factory where Seamus used to work. Even though Barbara complained that it was the most boring work in the world, she smiled as she waved her little brown pay packet in front of Amanda every Friday. Now that she could eat what she wanted, when she wanted, Amanda had started cooking and was surprised that she was so much better at it than her mum. All she needed to do, she saw, was to guard over the cooker, to make sure the beans or soup bubbled instead of boiled dry and that the veg was taken out of the water before it got too soft. As she got more adventurous, she used the recipes in her mum's magazines: curry and rice, green bean casserole, leek and potato soup, cauliflower cheese, garlic mushrooms that her mum had first eaten holding her nose. Every evening Barbara brought home food for the next day's meal and Amanda would unpack the bags and serve up what she'd made that day as her mother was washing upstairs. They would eat in front of the TV and Barbara would drink a glass or four of wine, letting her have a little bit. Barbara would talk over the news, her mouth crammed with food, telling Amanda the latest about the problems she was having with two women at work who were constantly giving her grief, calling them badly painted, big-mouthed tarts. Barbara told Amanda stories, of how the village looked when she was little, with its tea shop and the monkey grave that is still there now, by the bandstand. She talked of the cinema that used to be there, that she went to with her mother, sucking on butterscotch sweets as she watched the newsreels of the war. She talked of her father being called up so near the end, only they didn't know that of course, leaving her mother pregnant when he went, and how Barbara didn't meet him, on account of his being so badly injured, until she was almost nine, a stranger in the house that she never got used to. How he ruled the roost and made her do too much homework, how he cut up Aunty Pammy's miniskirts when she was out at work. She talked too, when she was half cut, of Seamus, about how much she hated his goddamn bitch of a mother.

'Do you remember,' she asked Amanda one time, 'when you were just a baby and you'd started walking for the first time? You'd just started doing it, that day, about two o'clock in the afternoon. When he got home, I showed him. I pushed you toward him and you started tottering away and you got across that room double quick, reaching out for him all the way.'

Barbara swigs at her glass and then lights a cigarette, handing the packet to Amanda.

'What happened?' Amanda said.

'He waited until you were almost by him. "Big deal," he said, and walked out of the room. And you were left there, looking at the door.'

Once Amanda tried to tell her mum about being yelled at in front of the class by dickhead Adams but she went 'mmm' because the music to Coronation Street had started and Amanda forgot about what she was saying and became glued, like her mother, to the TV.

Amanda tells her shrink how Gran and Grandad started coming round again, every Thursday. Gran made meat and potato pie that Aunty Pammy carried round in a glass bowl wrapped in layers of tea towel. After Grandad finished saying grace, everyone tucked in and there was no silence at the table anymore. Everyone talked for England from start to finish and nobody seemed to notice Amanda pushing all the little pellets of mince to the side of her plate. If anyone mentioned Belfast or the Falklands, Gran refused to listen and changed the subject while pretending to cover Amanda's ears.

'It's a new leaf for us all now,' she'd say.

Aunty Pammy has taken to going to the Asian shops in Rochdale and buying little treats for them each week. She brought almonds that she'd roasted in a tin with sugar, told to do that, she said, by the shopkeeper. When Amanda saw them, glistening like brown beetles in the bowl, she felt a thump of nausea. It happened more and more often now, when she looked at food: mashed potato or beef paste sandwiches or soup where the butter has slipped off the dipped bread and formed little slicks across the surface.

'No thanks, Aunty,' she said, and helped herself to a chocolate biscuit, trying to push the image of those oily ovals, slipping over each other, to the back of her mind.

'Has your mum got any better?' the shrink asks her.

'A bit.'

Amanda lies easily these days, says as little as possible, as neutrally as possible. She always looks at him when she lies, unable to tell if he believes her or not.

Two weeks ago, somebody rapped at the front door and Amanda jumped out of her skin, thinking it must be her dad at this time of night. Barbara was smiling though and Amanda heard Aunty Pammy chuckling, as if she were drunk.

'Where are you?' Aunty Pammy yelled. Amanda went into the kitchen and saw Mum and Aunty Pammy pushing each other like they were kids as they assembled bread and butter and ham on the table.

'What's happening?

'We're going to Manchester.'

'Why?'

'We're going to see the Pope,' Aunty Pammy said. 'He's saying Mass tomorrow, in Heaton Park. What do you think about that?'

'How will we get there?' Amanda says.

Aunty Pammy grabs her and dances her up and down the kitchen.

'Special buses from the town centre – special Catholic buses,' she sang as she moved. Amanda joined in the singing with her and they raced up and down, banging against the table and the cooker.

Her mum was watching and laughing and shaking her head as she packed sandwiches and malt loaf into plastic bags. They got a lift from Mr Emerson who played the organ for the church and his car smelt of Christmas trees which was nice at first but started to choke her after a few minutes. When he parked outside the town hall, Amanda was the first out of the car and she saw the line of buses with their headlights gleaming in the black of the night. People were stood around with bags and flasks and it was strange to see small children running about as if it was daytime. Gran and Grandad were already stood by the buses, with other people Amanda recognised from church.

'Here she is, our Mandy. What do you think of this then, eh? All of us gadding about in the middle of the night,' her gran said. Amanda sat with her gran on the front seats having begged them all to go upstairs. They'd all climbed up for her, even her gran who plonked herself down in her seat out of breath.

'Here's to our adventure. And praise to the Lord for bringing the summer at long last,' her gran said, and she raised an imaginary glass in the air. Amanda stood at the huge window and watched the road disappear underneath her. The bus went past rows of big houses and she wanted to see inside them but most were in darkness. There was just one with a light on and the curtains open and she saw a man chasing a woman around the sofa but the woman wasn't afraid, she was laughing. And the man was only in his underwear, which Amanda laughed at. When the bus left the houses behind and turned into an unlit road with fields at either side, she could only see dim shadows squatting in the darkness so she closed her eyes and snuggled up to her gran who felt cool against her. When she woke up, she felt as though she'd only been asleep for a minute but the bus was already at Manchester. She rubbed her eyes as she stumbled down the steps and out into the air that was still surprisingly warm. Heaton Park was vast. There were swarms of people everywhere, stretching so far that they blended into the darkness like shadows of ghosts and Amanda kept checking that her family were still beside her. There were lines of burger vans and candyfloss stalls at the gates and people sold necklaces that glowed in the dark. They found an empty spot and the women laid down layers of bin bags and blankets. Aunty Pammy handed Amanda another blanket to put round her legs later on and then she poured out tea for everyone. Amanda ate a cheese sandwich and looked at the people that surrounded her on all sides, stretching away until all she could see were the multicoloured neon dots. A hum of excitement vibrated in the night, as if the park itself were breathing.

The next morning Aunty Pammy woke them early and told them to get up so they could get a good view. They packed everything up and moved to the top of the hill that ran along the road the Pope would be driven down. They had a great spot right up against the railings, but Amanda's legs were aching, especially the back of the knees and she needed the toilet badly. Aunty Pammy kept saying 'any minute now'. Then a helicopter growled its way across the sky and the crowd hushed and watched it move, until it disappeared behind a line of trees and the growl died down to a purr. Eventually a cheer started on the right edge of the park and a minute later, the Pope Mobile appeared. It moved slowly along and the Pope was stood in the top, waving at everyone. The cheering got louder. He passed right in front of Amanda. Aunty Pammy and Mum started waving frantically and Gran and Grandad shouted 'Holy Father'. Amanda waved with them but she didn't cheer or call him any names. The Pope looked exactly the same as he did on the news and his robes were so white in the sunshine, they glowed. His robes looked heavy and Amanda wondered if he was too hot standing there waving. And then he moved past and the waving was all over and the crowd was already lumbering off towards the big stage where he would say Mass. They waited at the fence until a space cleared in front of them and then Aunty Pammy linked arms with Amanda and her mum and they followed Gran and Grandad back down the hill. They passed a man lying on the floor with an ambulance beside him. The ambulance had made tyre tracks in the grass. There is a long queue for the portable toilets and when Amanda finally got to it, the toilet stank so much she held her nose and hovered above the seat in case of germs. When she got out, Aunty Pammy had a plastic bottle of water that they all rinsed their hands in, but she could feel the dirt seeping down into her skin and she had to keep wiping them on her jeans.

Amanda saw them at the same time as her mother. They were stood at the back of the crowd but were trying to move to the front. Their faces were three quarters turned as they looked at each other talking and pointing to different paths through the throng. They were the right height, had the right colour hair, the right lankiness to the pair of them. One turned round for a second, as Barbara started shouting out their names, and blue eyes flashed before they both turned away and began to push once more at the crowd. She was running with her mum, both of them yelling now, and Amanda didn't care that people were staring and glaring and saying things, she pushed past the first few people in the crowd and there was the jacket of her brother and she could feel her mother behind her and she grabbed the jacket and a stranger turned. All the features were like Jamie's, the nose and the fringe flopping over one eye and the smile even, but the features had been moved here and there, the smile had slid down until it rested right on the chin, the hair had lightened itself.

And it was not him, not Jamie, nor Tommo, and she and her mother had to turn around and push back through the crowd.

'I want to go home,' her mum said, and nobody argued. They marched in opposite directions, Aunty Pammy and Gran and Grandad heading back towards the crowd and Amanda and her mum to the bus stop. Her mother started crying about halfway home. When they got back, Amanda helped her mum upstairs and put her straight to bed, tucking the bedspread around her as if she were a child.

Amanda looks at her shrink who is watching her with that intense stare of his.

'Are you okay?' he says. 'You don't seem okay. You seem very sad to me. Do you want to tell me a bit more?'

Amanda has nothing more to say. She is embarrassed to remember all she imagined, the birth of whatever it is that is trapped inside her. Whenever she thinks about home, about what she wanted after her dad left, and what she has got, she feels herself shut down. She floats, high above her body, a lot of the time now. Amanda is always running or hiding, like a fugitive. The absence of Jamie and Tommo is like a permanent stitch in her side and if she allows herself to think of them, she has the sensation that she is breaking into two halves that won't fit together again. Her mum has stopped talking since the Pope came and she gave up her job as well, saying she was sick of all the bloody nosy parkers sticking their beaks into her business. She now sits, as she has done every day for the past fortnight, silent in her armchair with a glass of wine in her hand and the breakfast Amanda still makes for her untouched on the floor beside her. A long line of ash usually dangles from her cigarette, which hangs from her other hand slung over the arm of the chair. Amanda used to talk to her, trying to coax something out in return, but she never answered so now Amanda doesn't speak either. The only sounds come from the kettle screeching or the toilet flushing, the clang of a spoon in a mug or her mum's slippers sliding across the dirty carpets as she moves from sofa to bed.

'I'd like you to tell me how you feel.'

'I'm always tired.'

'Are you sleeping any better?'

'Not really.'

Her nightmares have come back, worse than ever. She has to keep the light on at night and when she is finally on the cusp of sleep, her body jerks and her eyes fly open, scanning the tiny room for things she doesn't even believe in.

'Are you still having dreams?'

'Yep.'

'What happens in them?'

'I'm always hiding. I'm always really small.'

'Are those the worst ones?'

'They're not as bad as the dreams where I'm flying over everything, over the school and over the fields and everyone's looking for me but they can't see me and the wind is pulling me far away. I wake up fuckin'... sorry sir... wake myself up crying.'

'Have you got used to your medication now?'

'No, I hate it.'

She doesn't tell him that she hasn't taken it for months, that she takes each one off her mother and instead of taking it, adds it to the little pile under the radiator in the bedroom.

'Why is that? I thought it might have evened out by now?'

The tablets made everything feel unreal, like she's trapped in a nightmare. When she went outside at break times, she stayed by the wall, away from the hordes of kids who looked, out of the corner of her eye, like a single dark animal inching across the playground towards her, the laughing and screaming and shouting all smashing together until she wanted to cover her ears. She watched as other kids joined the crowd, blending into the uniformed camouflage and they looked like they were dissolving before her eyes, melting away into the heaving mass.

'I don't know.'

'What happened with the teaching? You said at the meeting you thought it would be good.'

That school meeting had dragged on for almost two hours, time considered wasted by the look on the headmistress' face, who said little except to remind everyone that they had taken her in when no other school would, as if she were talking about a stray dog. Her mother said nothing throughout, nodded her head at whoever was talking. The others – the Wacky Man, the shrink, Mr K – recited what they seemed to have said a dozen or more times before, talking of her qualities, of being gifted, her fierce intelligence, a list of attributes that a thing, unlike a human, has no use for. When they asked her if she would be a reading mentor two hours a week, she agreed because, like her mother, she is used to nodding at whoever is looking at her. She has done only two remedial reading classes. The boy she is teaching is in the year below her and he is still reading books she had completed before finishing primary school. At the first session she sat with Miss Price, who showed her how to help him. On the second session she is alone with him and he is struggling with the word 'tunnel'.

'Put your finger over the second part of the word,' she tells him, and he does this. 'Read what the first part says.'

'Tun.'

'Now put your finger over the first part of the word.'

'Nel.'

'Put the two together.'

'What?'

'Tun-nel,' she says.

'Tun-nel, tun-nel, tun-nel,' he repeats.

'You know? Tunnel.'

'Yep. Tunnel.'

When Miss Price leaves the room to get a cup of tea, the boy turns to her and whispers, 'Everyone says you're a fucking psycho.'

She whispers back, 'You're fucking illiterate and you don't even know what illiterate means, you, thick, stupid cunt.'

Miss Price comes back and beams at the two of them hunched over the book.

'I'm going home now,' Amanda says, and she is out of the door before Miss Price has had a chance to say anything. She runs home and inside lets her face change; lets the colour rise and the tears slip. Later she goes downstairs, finds bacon in the fridge, and some stale bread that she toasts, pours hot water onto three spoons of coffee and takes a weaker cup into her mother who doesn't ask her why she is home early, just accepts the proffered drink. They sit together watching *Armchair Theatre*, about an assassin with a poison dart hidden inside an umbrella. When Amanda takes one of her mother's cigarettes, her mother says nothing, just tuts, as if to herself, and stares at the screen.

'Earth to Amanda!'

Amanda comes round as if she were asleep. She shakes her head a little, shifts in her chair and tries to sit up straight.

'Amanda? What happened with the teaching?'

'I didn't like it.'

'Why is that?'

'I'm no good at it.'

'But what do you do instead, when you're not at school?'

'I read. Watch TV. Sometimes I take Bonnie for a walk.'

'Where do you go?'

'That would be telling. I don't want the Wacky Man knowing where I go.'

She thinks of old Mr Wilson laying in wait behind a tree up by the reservoir, hobbling out to try and drag her to school.

'I'm just kidding. I go up to the reservoir.'

'What do you do up there?'

'I just sit by the water, watch the dog paddling.'

Amanda can see Bonnie poking a paw gingerly into the water. Sometimes the dog slips on the stones at the edge and goes flying, plunges into the water and then swims frantically back to the edge and always comes to stand right by her before shaking the water off, as she jumps up and tries to get out of the way. She sits again and feels how differently time ticks on up there. At home her mind is like a policeman in the middle of a busy crossroad, thoughts flying at her from all directions, veering off just as she thinks they'll all come crashing into her. Here she can close her eyes and see nothing emerging from shadowy corners, can listen to nothing but the slap of water against the bank, Bonnie panting softly as she scratches at dried-out cowpats. No thoughts chase her up here, nothing nipping at her but the wind. She never knows how long she sits. Long enough for the knots inside her to loosen, long enough to feel smoothed out.

'Amanda, are you listening?'

'Sorry, what did you say?'

'What books do you read?'

'Mum's Catherine Cookson books or her *Reader's Digest* magazines. And she's got about four *National Geographic*s in the bottom of one of her drawers. I've read them loads. Tommo's encyclopedias – they're my favourite. There's so much in there, I forget loads of stuff. It's always like I'm reading them for the first time.'

'What does your mum do?'

'She's asleep a lot of the time, in bed. Sometimes I make dinner for her. If she gets up to eat it we watch TV together.'

'Do you talk to your mum?'

'Not much. I tell her we need food and stuff, write notes for the shop for her. Most of the time I'm in my bedroom.'

'Why is that?'

'My aunty comes round every afternoon after she's finished work and then she tells me to go and play, as if I'm still fucking – sorry for swearing, Mr Broeder – ten years old or something. She's always talking to Mum, on and on about my brothers, so I just go up in my bedroom to read or something.'

'So you were angry with them? Is that why you keep fighting at school?'

'People keep saying shit to me all the time.'

'What things are they saying?'

She bites her fingernails, one after the other. She wants to tell him that school is like being in the Middle Ages, that she might as well be taken through the streets on a fucking cart, everyone jeering.

'Can you tell me about it?'

'It's just stuff, stupid stuff, all the time. I want to be left alone, not dragged into school where they put me in classes with big-mouthed idiots who can barely write their own fucking names. Sorry for swearing.'

He never says anything about her swearing. He never interrupts her either, once she starts to speak. He sits up in his chair or and nods encouragement and Amanda thinks she has said too much.

'Have you heard from your dad?'

'He sent Mum another letter.'

Seamus' first letter came a few months after he left. Amanda saw it on the kitchen table, a pale blue rectangle half out of its matching envelope, when her mum went to pay the milkman. She read it through, correcting the spelling mistakes in her head as she went. Her dad asked after her mum and said he hoped the letter finds her and Grace and James all well and that he hoped the money was enough for bills and food and such. He finished with *I meant what I said. This will be a new start for us.* He's signed it *Ever, Seamus* and squashed into the little space below his name he'd written *You can bring the girl.* Amanda spat at his scrawled name, screwed the paper into a ball and dropped it in her mum's half-empty tea mug. Her mum had finally written back, prompted by Aunty Pammy and Gran, that they weren't going to live in Ireland, that they couldn't leave their family behind and that she, Barbara, needed to wait here for when the boys finally came home. There was no reply for months and then one day, Amanda asked her mum for money to buy food for tea and had her head bitten off. When she asked what was wrong, Barbara threw another letter at her, yelling,

'There isn't any more money.' This letter had no greeting in it, just words scratched deep into cheap paper.

You're on your own now. And don't think that you can get yourself a fancy man. If I hear about you behaving like a whore, I'll come over there and burn the fucking house down with you two in it.

It was after that letter that everything finally collapsed at home. Amanda thinks of how her mum hardly leaves her dad's old chair. How they're always running out of baked beans and bread and toothpaste and toilet roll. She thinks of the notes for the shop she's forged, because she can't get her mum to do anything. She writes them onto bits of paper torn from the fronts or backs of her mum's paperbacks which she hands to Specky Kev who glances at them before he goes off to gather bacon and milk and golden grain bread. He is not supposed to serve kids cigarettes but he never says anything. She thinks of the way they have had to rent a TV since the old one broke, and how they never have 50p for it anyway. Amanda has learned to poke a knife into the coin slot at the back and waggle it about until something makes a loud ticking noise and then the TV crackles back into life. Her mum shouted at her for doing that at first, but now, as with everything, she says nothing at all. If she set herself on fire her mum would just sit there looking at her. Amanda thinks of the way newspapers are piled behind the armchair and inside the sideboard, the way the dust lies thick along the cabinet shelves and the mantelpiece and the TV stand, the way the paint is starting to peel off some of the windows now her dad is no longer there to maintain them, and the corner of wallpaper that has come unstuck in the kitchen. She thinks of the dog hair that is spreading like a second carpet and how the hoover, unused since something clogged the tube, is stacked up alongside heaps of bags and boxes in the cupboard under the stairs, which is so jam-packed they can't get in to see what's inside. She thinks of the meals she conjures out of tins and packets and the washing up she does that gleams like jewellery among the grubbiness. She thinks of the way in which her aunty keeps on at her mum, as she tries to tidy up around her, until her mother shouts for her to stop mithering. And she thinks of the last time she saw her gran, when she came round one day to check on them, ruffling Amanda's hair as if she were still five years old as she spoke to Barbara.

'You have to listen to me. You can't go on like this. You have to get up, get yourself dressed.'

Barbara doesn't answer her. She doesn't look at her mother, just pulls her dressing gown around her and stares at the half-closed curtains.

'Come on. Get up and get yourself dressed. And I'll help you sort out the house. You have to pull yourself together. Think of Amanda, do you not think she's been through enough?'

'And what about me? Haven't I been through enough, for Christ's sake?'

'She's only a child. And the worst is over now, love. Time for a new start for you and Mandy. Everyone at church is asking after you love. You go have a bath while I tidy things up in here. It will do you the world of good.'

'And once I've had that bath? Then what, exactly? Shall I tart myself up and go outside with the whole bloody place talking about me? Pitying me for putting up with everything all those years and having nothing at all to show for it? For having no idea where my boys are? When they ask me how I am, what shall I say? That I'm not so bad considering that my husband's friends are telling everyone he's going to divorce me so he can marry some other bloody idiot? Shall I come to Mass with you and tell all your bloody, goddamn, fucking Catholic friends *that*? You know what? You can take your help and fucking *shove* it.'

Amanda watches her gran leave, hears the metal click of the front door's lock that makes exactly the same sound as when her gran snaps the big gold clasp on her handbag shut. And then she watches her mum stumble over the breakfast plate, standing on her uneaten toast, before storming out of the room and up the stairs, leaving a trail of minuscule butter spots on the floor behind her.

'What are you favourite memories, from when you were younger?' Mr Broeder asks.

'I liked it when I was sick,' Amanda tells him.

'You liked being sick?'

'Yeah. I got to stay at Gran's house, so my mum could get on with the housework.'

'Was that nice?'

'It was gorgeous.'

She would lie on the couch and her gran would warm coats by the fire and then lay them on top of her, each layer tightly tucked over her, their warm weight pressing down. She became a creature in a burrow, safe, warm, sleepy. She would be wakened gently at lunchtime and eat if she could, then she'd help her gran put food out for the birds and they'd watch them feeding for a while before she went back to the coats, snoozing under them with half-formed pictures from her gran's stories of the old days, fever hospitals and electric trams floating across her mind. And her gran taught her card games. They played Gin Rummy and Fish and then when her gran went to cook, she played Patience non-stop, trying not to rush but to look carefully like gran had taught her, as she waited for the knock at the door that meant her mother had come to take her home.

'Do you miss her?'

She wants to say to him, 'What the fuck do *you* think?' She finds some of his questions ridiculous and it makes her angry, but she reins it in. After all, it's because she's such a fucking nutcase that she has to go have her head examined every week. And she doesn't miss her dad one iota, so how would he know who and what she misses?

'What are you thinking about?' he asks her.

'I'm not thinking anything really. I mean, I'm thinking about too much to think about just one thing.'

'What do you mean?'

'It's like when Dad overfilled the bin so the lid didn't fit and then the wind blew it right off and all the rubbish at the top came flying out, the chippy wrappers and plastic bags and the crisp packets me and Tommo had hidden, all spinning about in the air. And then the wind stopped for a bit and it all fell towards the ground, but then the wind started again and blew it all over the place. My thoughts are like that.'

'That's an excellent description Amanda. We've almost finished for today. Do you want to tell me anything else?'

Amanda wants to tell her shrink that she thinks about her gran all the time, who still won't step foot in the house since the argument because Barbara refuses to apologise, wants to say how much she misses her and wants to go stay with her again. And how, every time she wakes up, she has to check that her mother hasn't done what she is always saying she will do, but is still breathing in the bed or chair.

'Where do you come from, Mr Broeder?'

He sits and looks at her and he smiles, showing those pointy teeth.

'I'm from the Netherlands.'

'How many languages can you speak?'

'Three. Dutch and English and a little French.'

'Okay.'

'Anything else?'

'No.'

'I will see you next week then. Are you going to try to go to school tomorrow?'

'Yes,' she lies.

Normally the very mention of school sets her teeth on edge, has her fingers reaching up to rub and pull at her hair, but right now there is no room in her head for school – she is thinking about how she will get home. She has to go outside where anyone and everyone can see her, where they might sense her madness through her blazing eyes and bitten fingernails and her pig-face and malformed body. The journey is overwhelming. She has to break it into tiny steps to stop it crushing her. Leave Mr Broeder's office. Go to the door in reception. Open it. Step outside. Walk to the bus station. Wait in the queue. Get money ready. Move forward as people board the bus. Check money. Get on the bus. Don't trip up the step. Pay the driver and grab a ticket. Say thanks. Go to the back, downstairs (never upstairs because school is now over and kids could be lurking in their animalistic packs). Sit in the corner on the right. Don't think about the germs filling up the bus with every breath of everybody on here. Don't touch anything with bare hands. Keep the jacket sleeves wrapped over fingers. Don't make eye contact. Watch the landmarks go past – the church in the middle of the roundabout, the coach station, the hospital at the top of the hill. Only two stops now to go. Get off the bus. Don't trip down the step. Turn right off the bus, up Eyelees Road. Move as fast as possible. Turn left and up into Mill Road. Turn right into the snicket with the high fences. Speed up here – start running where nobody can see you lurching along. Watch the path for dog shit. Run out the other side and across the road to the house. Open the garden gate. Hold it up on the right side where it's broken. Don't trip up the steps. Open the door. Don't look round. Get in the house. Close door. Pant, doubled up, until breath comes back. Safe.

'Bye, Amanda,' her shrink says. 'See you next week.'

'See ya.'

She pulls her denim jacket around her and opens the door, dips a toe outside as if paddling in the sea, tells herself to start moving.

Amanda hasn't gone to school again. She really meant to this time but as she reached the gate, she remembered that she's not fed her rabbits for days. She has four rabbits now, despite Barbara telling her she couldn't have any more. The two new ones were given to her by the neighbour's son up the road. The stink of urine-soaked straw hits her as she goes into the shed, and the straw is so wet it's turned the droppings into a mush that the rabbits are covered in. The new rabbits are both pure white, except they now seem like a dirty grey-brown. Amanda tells them she's sorry and begins to sort them out. She takes out the all the margarine tubs she uses for food and water and cleans them on an old towel she keeps there. She rinses them with one of the bottles of water she's brought. Then she puts the two white rabbits into the corner of the shed and drags out the filthy straw. As she moves the first heap she sees funny little forms littered through the yellow strands. They are pastel pink and seem to almost glow. She picks one up and rubs the straw off it. It is the same shape and colour as the sugar shrimps she likes to eat but when she looks again she sees it is a rabbit foetus. The straw is full of them. She throws it down and screams and the rabbits all start bucking in their cages. She stands there for a while, her eyes glued to the straw that lays half in and half out of a plastic bag, decorated with dead babies. She runs back to the house and sits in the front room where she tries to push out the picture of that creature she just held in her hand, translucent with black dot eyes. Eventually she goes back wearing her mum's washing-up gloves. She collects the straw together and stuffs it into a bin bag that she takes to the dustbin. She then opens the shed door and puts all the rabbits outside where they hop around for a while and then start to make their way back to the shed. She claps her hands, hard, twice and the noise rings in the cold morning air. The rabbits bolt for the hedge and she watches them make their way through two of the neighbours' gardens. She takes the food and water bottles and puts them on top of the plastic bags and puts the dustbin lid on, ramming it down until it stays put.

She would like to tell her brothers about this. She wants them to poke fun at her about it, even chase her around with closed fists that they say they have the dead babies inside, to give her a dead arm or a Chinese burn or to let her go tree climbing with them even though they will try to push her out of it. She goes into the house and into their old bedroom and she pokes around in the closets and smells the clothes they left behind. She finds the box under the bottom bunk that used to be Tommo's bed. It is newly placed there, by her mum. Amanda knows this because she is always poking around in their room, but hasn't seen the box before. Inside it is a half-dozen of her brothers' old comics, two sets of Trump cards and Tommo's old pocket calculator, the one that plays a musical note for each number you press. At the bottom is a picture with her and her brothers in it, taken in the back garden, Jamie and Tommo's arms wrapped around each other, her at the side of her brothers with Bonnie crouching at her feet. Her mum is sat in a chair in a swimsuit reading a newspaper. She looks again at her brothers, their eyes crinkled against the sun, and then at herself, stood out of the glare. They all look as if they have been frozen far longer than the taking of the picture, as if they had been motionless long before the photo was taken, might well be motionless long after. The three of them are similarly small and thin, elbows and knees sticking out from cuffs and hems. She thinks of them back then, like the rabbits she's just let go, always watching for danger, their ears pricking constantly where they sat or stood, six blue eyes darting to and fro as they played. Amanda pushes the memory back inside herself, holds it, along with the photo, at arm's length. In the picture they know nothing of what is to come, still have years together before Tommo and Jamie will march away to freedom.

'Little fucking animals,' she says to them and rips the photo in two, lets the pieces fly out of her hand onto the carpet.

The new school skirt, that Aunty Pammy bought her, is long enough but far too tight across her stomach. Period pains stab inside and it feels as if her stomach swells with each pulse of pain. She has cut old clothes into squares that she uses for sanitary towels and she wonders if her mother has even thought about it. She has never asked her about it and Amanda is both relieved and angry that she hasn't. She wants to know that it is all normal, that there isn't something wrong inside her. She is too embarrassed to ask, and the bleeding disgusts her; it is painful and dirty and savage, it makes her feel like a mutant, a cave woman. The skirt clings to her stomach and then sticks out like a tent from her hips to her knees and her legs are on display. Even wearing long socks she feels exposed, everyone will be looking at her huge fat legs. Almost all the other girls roll their skirts up and their socks down, or they have lacy ankle socks. And they all wear these little black or purple pointy shoes with bows across the front. She has horrible square shoes that look like she is wearing black boxes on her feet. She tried her basketball boots, but they make the skirt look even more ridiculous. She put her jeans back on and her baggy black jumper that reaches down past her thighs and over her hands, covering the bitten nails. She goes downstairs and throws the skirt on the sofa.

'It's too tight, I can't wear it. I'm not going.'

Her mother looks at her for a long time, eventually says, 'How can it be too tight?'

'By being too fucking small. I can't wear it.'

'You can't wear your jeans to school.'

'I'm not going to school.'

'You have to go. You promised Mr Kramm. He's worked his backside off to get permission for you.'

Amanda is sick of the interventions, as they call them. Every time one fails and she thinks they've given up, another one pops up. She wants them to give up on her, it would be easier all round. She imagines trying to get from the school gate to the English class on the other side, where everyone can see the way she is, moon-faced and monstrous. Laughing at her because nothing is the shape it ought to be, her nose too big and thick, her eyes too round, her face too big and white, arms and legs like tree trunks. Her fingers, pudgy and bloodied at the ends where she bites them, look like raw sausages. She can see herself, striding so fast that her calves cramp, her arms folded against her chest and the feeling that she can't breathe hits her so hard that she doubles up and puts her hand onto the back of the sofa so she doesn't fall. She sees her mother watching her, her face showing that she thinks what she is seeing is a pantomime.

'I'm not fucking going.'

'Oh, for Christ's sake. You wouldn't have dared speak to your dad like that.'

'Well, he's not here – and you obviously weren't there when I fucking did speak to him like that.'

'That's right, keep reminding me that I'm the one left with all the bloody mess to sort out.' Amanda stands biting on a finger while the pain in her belly fires up again.

'Why do you have to be so bloody difficult?'

'Why? Why do you fucking think?'

Barbara picks up the skirt, throws it at her. Amanda catches the skirt, takes it in both hands and rips it. It gives way more easily than she thought it would, ripping all the way along the seam to the hem, the zip detached on one side.

'You stupid little bitch,' Barbara says, 'money went on that skirt.'

'Stupid bitch yourself.' Amanda runs upstairs and closes the door, takes the bit of razor from inside the top drawer and she drags it across the skin on her forearm again and again, cross hatching the lines so that a lattice of blood rises and begins to run. When she hears her mother at the door, she drops the razor quickly and lowers her jumper sleeve.

'Get up and go to school. You can wear your bloody jeans.'

'I hate it there. I'm not going.'

'Fuck it. See if I care. You can sit there all bloody day.'

Her mother slams the door and stomps back downstairs. Amanda sits on her bed and looks out the window, sees girls from her school walking down the road together, slim and neat in their uniforms. One of them looks up and sees her and waves, and she jumps back as if they can see the mess on her arm. She closes the curtains but she feels exposed, as if prying eyes can see right through the flimsy cloth, so she sits on the floor under the windowsill with her back to the radiator. She picks up a book and reads for a while but she can't remember what she's read and has to keep going back to the same page. She lights a cigarette and goes downstairs to the kitchen to see what she can find to eat. She thinks she can hear Jamie and Tommo, calling her name the way they used to, softly so that Seamus won't hear. She opens the fridge door. As she passes the front room with two pieces of bread half ripped by lumps of cheese spread, she looks through the crack under the hinges of the door and sees her mother sat in Dad's old chair, a hand on either arm of it, looking straight ahead as tears stream down her face. She stuffs a piece of the bread and cheese into her mouth and goes back to her bedroom. She lights another cigarette and takes deep drags that make the racing thoughts dissolve into nothing. As she stretches to flick the ash, she feels the pull of a single hair that is caught somehow by the radiator. It sends an itch like an electric shock to one tiny little part of her head. She feels above her head with her hands and finds the hair, raised up with static, and she gets it between her fingers and pulls. The hair comes out with a delicious pop that she feels deep inside her ears at the same time that the tiny itch ripples along her head. She sits there all morning, lighting cigarette after cigarette. In between each drag she pulls out her hair – pop, pop, pop.

Amanda has been watching out for the Wacky Man, who has been coming every day for the past three months. She had almost picked up where she left off, allowed to wear her jeans and jacket and settling without any problem in terms of studying, but then on the way to metalwork class she forgot not to look at her reflection in the windows running along the corridor. She saw her face, a blob of bright white, as if it were bleached. She stopped in her tracks to look at the thing in the window and then she kicked it. The safety glass juddered slightly, the little wires inside it shimmering, and she watched the thing dance. Adams appeared from nowhere, his eyes piggish behind his thick glasses.

'I might have guessed it would be you, Duffy, you waste of bloody space. Stop that.'

Amanda turned away and ran along the corridor.

'Did I give you permission to move? Get back here, thug.'

Amanda stuck two fingers up in the space behind her shoulder. She was just inside the main doors when he caught her, had just thrown them open on their well-oiled hinges making them boom loudly against their frame like claxons announcing her attempted escape. He grabbed her by the shoulders, his fingers digging down into her flesh, and then he rammed her against the wall, three times, before he let go, letting her drop to the floor. She was up on her feet before he's even halfway turned, screaming and whirling around him trying to land blows and kicks. The headmistress's office was situated, like a gatekeeper's cottage, right by the exit and

198

when she appeared at her window, shaking her fist in the air like a cartoon, Amanda ran for home. When she reached the bottom of the hill, she passed some friends of her gran who shouted hello as if she was strolling past rather than running. When she got home, she went into the front room to show her mum the marks.

Amanda started to tell her what happened but Barbara shoved a hand right in her face.

'I've heard it all already. I don't want to know,' she said, 'I no longer care.'

'Fuck you then,' Amanda said.

She had an urge to pull at her mother's hair, to pull any more of those words right out of her head but then she saw her mum's glassy-eyed stare. Amanda wanted her mum to smile at her and say that Gran is coming round and that their freedom, so long in coming, isn't too heavy for them to carry and that the house, with just them in it, hasn't died. When her mum said nothing more, just sat there looking tired with shadows under her eyes, Amanda almost said sorry, but her mum turned away as the words were still forming inside her mouth.

The Wacky Man always arrives at the same time each morning but today he is late. Amanda looks through the tiny gap she's made in the curtains. She couldn't sleep last night so passed the time thinking of all of the things she will talk about with him today and she is struggling to retain them all because she's been on the lookout and her stomach is making sloshing sounds and cramping up. It is gone one o'clock in the afternoon because she heard the faint bell of the proddy-dog church over by the graveyard. Just as she thinks he isn't coming, she sees him walking up the white path. She quickly wipes her eyes and runs to the door, taking the stairs three steps at a time.

'What's happened? To stop you going to school?' he asks.

She thinks about the looks she saw in Mr Adams' eyes, that same look her dad had every time he laid into her, and she thinks of the men she sees everywhere, with these same eyes, waiting to turn their fists into wrecking balls. She can't tell the Wacky Man this any more than she could explain why her ability to go outside is fragile as a snowflake, has melted away to leave her trapped, as if there an invisible barrier, a magnetic field across the front door. When she tries to step outside, her whole body shakes and her heart swells up until it's too big in her chest and she feels like it will burst out and land on the grass in the garden. When she opens the front door the outside stretches out in front of her, the space is too vast and blinding. She feels lost under those big white clouds and blue sky.

She wants to tell the Wacky Man about how before, the feeling was something small and she could think of something she wanted to do outside and squashing the feeling would be easy, but now the feeling is so huge it squashes her instead. There is too much to say and too many words to choose from and none of them fit what she wants to say anyway, human words to describe non-human things. So she clamps down all he's stirred up, masks the feelings that writhe under the surface. She watches him shake his head with a face full of understanding, that kind smile never faltering. She wants to speak, to confess all the secret feelings that she holds inside. But she sees his eyes move over her grubby clothes, unwashed since the washing machine broke weeks back, and she imagines him as a young child, pushed around a garden on a wooden toy by a father who teases him in the same soft voice, or who holds him above his shoulders so he can play at being a giant. She sees the Wacky Man's thoughts of her – the lost cause – in the black of his pupils. She can't tell him about all these crazy thoughts and visions and she is suddenly tired of their conversation, tired of having to stand before people's glaring pity, has to fight an urge to slam the door in his face.

'I need to go to the loo, sir,' she says.

'Okay. I'll call in tomorrow.'

He walks down the path and turns, as he always does, to wave, but Amanda has already closed the door. The next day when he comes, at his usual time, Amanda, who was sat on the edge of her bed, anticipating his first knock, sinks to the floor beneath the windowsill. She hears her mum swearing from her bed but knows she won't get up, never rousing herself before afternoon these days. The knocking gets louder and she hears him calling her through the letterbox. She pulls at her hair as she waits for him to leave.

Amanda spent her last days downstairs reading or looking through her brother's old atlas and smoking if she could find any cigarettes. She usually had the TV on too, jemmying the coin slot so she could watch the old black-and-white films of women in long lacy dresses, glamorous and brooding and smoking through cigarette holders as terrible music crashed around in the background, or the odd little dramas about cults and espionage or adulterous couples murdering spouses in the way of the affair. The last time she heard her mum lumbering down the stairs, Barbara had appeared in the doorway before Amanda had torn her eyes away from the TV.

'Do you want a brew?' Amanda asked. Her mum had stared at her, without speaking, and then went into the kitchen. She returned with a mug of watery-looking tea that slopped over the side as she half fell into the chair.

'What's wrong, Mum?' Amanda asked her.

'What's wrong? What's fucking right?' her mother said, spilling more of her tea as she slammed it down onto the hearth. Her fingers scrabbled around the floor by her feet until she found her cigarette packet. She lit one and sat looking into space as she sucked the smoke into her mouth.

'Shall I make you some dinner?' Amanda asked.

Her mum didn't answer, just kept pulling on her fag as smoke poured from her nostrils as if she were a dragon.

'What should I do, Mum?' Amanda's voice was smaller and younger than it has been for a long time, for years, perhaps.

'I'll tell you what you can do. You can piss off and leave me alone.'

Amanda loitered in the doorway.

'Are you deaf? I don't want to set eyes on you, all this trouble you keep causing, without any bloody end to it. Get out of my goddamn sight.'

Amanda now stays in her room. Once Barbara calmed down, she kept asking Amanda to come out but she has stayed put, safe behind her bedroom door, out of the way of Barbara's words, hurled like knives. Barbara leaves her meals and drinks, with cigarettes, outside the door. God only knows, Amanda thinks, how long she will remember to feed her.

They've all been today, her teacher, her Wacky Man, her shrink, talking to her through the door, asking if she is alright, if she will let them help her. Her mother has placed a chair outside the room, so that they can sit, instead of squatting or standing. The thought of this makes her laugh out loud, even though her arms hurt, swollen with the cuts that cross her arms from wrist to elbow in thin, half-septic lines, even though every time she wakes and sees that she is still inside this dirty cell her fingers reach immediately for her hair. They arrive at the door in turn and speak to her. She doesn't answer any of them. When Mr K asks her if she liked her books, she thinks of the way she used to talk to him about anything and everything, how she needed to talk to him. Now she only scratches into her leg with the shard of mirror that has sticky smears of congealed blood on its point and she says nothing, even when he whispers through the door.

'Terry, can you hear me?'

Eventually he goes away again, and she feels every step he makes on the stairs but she still can't call out to him because she knows now that books can't bring her back. Mr Broeder sounds calm, dropping his words in a neat pile outside the door for her, but she opens the door a crack to listen to him talking to her mum in a new urgent voice, hears snippets of the 'arrangements'. He is saying she will be taken somewhere where she can be helped. She hears her mother's answers, the flat tone of her responses as if she were hearing updates about the weather. When her mother brought the food to the door yesterday, she told Amanda in that same dull voice, that she is bored of it now, exhausted by the constant letters from the school, all the bloody questions and the relentless knocking at the door. She told her that she is sick to death of everything and she'll walk out the door soon enough and not come back and then Amanda can just come out of her bloody room or starve to death. Amanda stopped being scared of this, on the surface anyway, a long time ago, the same way she is no longer scared that her dad will push a lighted rag through the letterbox. Her dad has forgotten that they exist and her mum is no more able to walk out the door than she is.

It is only at night that she can't shake off the feeling that he might just come. That he might have woken up one day and decided to come back. That he is someone who could easily ease open the gate, and sneak up the path with petrol in one hand and matches in the other. And her mum is downing a bottle of whatever each night, then falling into a deep sleep, oblivious to any possible dangers lurking in the dark. So she stays awake at night, anyway, just in case.

When she first shut herself away, she could tell what time of day it was from the muted noise pressing through the closed window: the milkman first, then the footsteps and hellos of the first of the people going to work at around seven o'clock, except for those who work in the local factory who set off around seven forty. Then the older kids going to school who start out from eight fifteen to half past and it's all talking and joking and running about. The little kids come after that, the mums gossiping and shouting. The postman turns up at the same time – and if there is a dog out, especially Bonnie, the postman starts yelling and you can hear his shoes slapping against the road and the mad barking following him. It goes quiet then, for ages, except for a burst of conversation here and there as housewives meet on the way to or from the shops, or the occasional rug having the living daylights beaten out of it in one of the gardens. She sometimes falls asleep for a while, woken up by factory people coming home for their lunch, noisier this time, raucous laughing and shouting to each other and then the sudden quiet as the houses envelope them. Half an hour later they go back to work and then it's quiet again, just the occasional knock of a salesman, the upward drift of words too soft to hear when someone answered their door. The afternoon exodus began at two forty five exactly, when the mums march down to bring back the little kids and hot on their heels the older school kids come home. It's all noise from then on: playing games, shouting, yelling, fighting, crying, mums coming out and demanding to know whose bloody fault it is this time. Shouts that tea is ready is rolled out from house to house followed by a short hiatus whilst food is swallowed or pushed to the side of plates. Then it's the long soundlessness that will stretch through the distance to the next dawn.

Now it's merely background noise. She doesn't go for walks in her head any more either. She used to walk everywhere, to the reservoir with Bonnie trotting beside her, to the library for books and the shop to buy bananas and bread cakes and bacon-flavoured crisps. She felt again the freshness of the air in the hills, the rain on her face and the springiness of the field grass under her trainers. She used to go to places out of books and atlases. She ambled through the markets of Madrid and the galleries of Amsterdam, took a train through France and a ferry to the tip of Africa. She looked upon the world's most famous art, architecture, ancient ruins and wildlife. In these walks she wore bright colours, she was pretty and thin and her face was normal. She walked with her head held high and the sun on her face. Now she realises how pathetic it was to think up a life, so she does nothing, just sits, supine in the stillness, listening to silence until her head screams with static. Her hands no longer pull out her hair but lie, white and scaly on her lap, like two dead fish.

She saw a news item, just before she closed her bedroom door against the world. A huge crowd of Indians swarming outside a run-down hut, clamouring to see the child inside that had been born with four arms, pressing forward when the family brought it out to try and touch its feet. She feels like that now, here, behind her door, the three wise men on a pilgrimage to save themselves by saving her, desperate for her to open the door, to reveal herself to them. The clamouring Indians believed the child to be a god, the hut a shrine, but when she watched them attack the tiny form, ripping at its gown, half crushing it as it screamed with fear, she knew it wasn't lucky at all, just another poor deformed bastard, just another freak in another show.

Part Eight
Disintegration

．．

Look who it isn't.

Yes, that was me screaming. Because I felt like it, that's why. When I feel like I'm going to burst, I scream. Except I don't really feel like it's me. It's like another me, inside, that wants to scream and I can't stop it. I feel like I'm watching the other me doing it, gliding above myself like a plane circling a trapped animal, like I have no control over the me that is screaming. You don't have to stare at me like that, I know I'm mental. Much more of this solitary confinement and I'll be eating fucking spiders and pulling out my teeth like Papillon. What? What's Papillon? It's a he, not a what. Steve McQueen? Dustin Hoffman? Never mind. Anyway, there you have it – my dad. He came here, set up his little dysfunctional nuclear unit, fucked it all up, made my brothers run away and drove me and Mum mad, and then he didn't want us anymore and he fucked off back to Ireland. And here I am, mind like a motorway pile up, thoughts all smashed up and sticking out of my brain. Aunty Pammy saw me this morning. I didn't know she was visiting – she must have made it up with Mum. I can't hear anything cos my ears arc all blocked up. They're fucking killing me as well. Anyway, I went to the toilet and there she was, helping Mum to move the old broken mirror out of her bedroom. I almost bumped into her and I jumped back and I saw her gasp as she looked at me, tears instantly filling her eyes, probably from the way I smell. Then I saw myself in the mirror – looked like my head was split in half with two long flaps of hair either side. Whiter than anything

I'd seen before. Eyes red and puffy, one closed up a bit. Aunty Pammy kept trying to hug me and I kept wriggling away from her, but she pinned my arms against me and in the end I was too tired to push her away so I just stood there with my eyes squeezed shut.

So they've all been to see me today. The shrink was here this afternoon, talking to me through the door like it's totally fucking normal. He said my heart is scared and that's why I feel tired a lot. He said the heart is like a seed and the food and water for it are positive words and good actions. That it wasn't my fault my heart was like this, and that they're going to help me get my heart working – 'blossoming, like a flower,' he said. And then he said that my dad had broken bits of me but that he could help me fix it all up. He said the Japanese fix broken things with gold, fill up all the cracks and chips with all this gold. He said they have a word for it – what was it? Oh yeah, *kintsugi* – and that they consider the fixed stuff to be more beautiful than the original. He said they usually mean cups and vases but that it applies to me too. Well, he was wrong, wasn't he? My cracks and chips are filled with gunk. I'm fucking filthy. Don't touch me – you'll get fucking dysentery. I'm a broken-down wreck. When someone breaks their leg, if it's not fixed, they hobble for the rest of their life. My head is hobbling. I've got some psychology of my own – if you are not wanted when you are born, the world will never want you.

I'm hungry but I can't eat. I keep thinking about tomorrow. I'm not shifting – they'll have to shoot me with a dart, like the animal that I am. I'm sick of oven chips anyway. Did I tell you about that time I snuck downstairs when Mum had gone somewhere and forgotten to put out my breakfast? It was months and months ago now, maybe a year back. I can't remember. I waited all day but she didn't come back and then at night I started panicking. I kept thinking she'd finally gone, done a runner at last and left me here. So eventually

I went downstairs. The house had loads of new noises that I'd not heard inside my bedroom. The hall was filthy. It looked as bad as my bedroom. There was dust and dog hair everywhere and old papers and letters all over the floor. The hoover was trapped in the corner and there were piles of old clothes – mine and Mum's – all around it. The front room was even worse, newspapers everywhere and plastic bags full of rubbish and coupons and greasy chip papers. Dirty cups too, stacked on their sides on the top of dirty plates and overflowing ashtrays. The curtains and windows in every room were as closed as mine and the whole house stank of cigarettes. I can remember when Mum didn't even smoke but now the stench was everywhere. I could *taste* it, stronger than anything upstairs and the top of the walls were all stained with it. It looked like there was a dirty yellow fog hanging under the ceilings. And Bonnie went bananas when I opened the kitchen door, jumping up and trying to lick my face. It was really nice. Mum came through the back door just as I'd stuffed my face with some cornflakes and we just looked at each other for ages. I couldn't believe how old she looked, she had lines going down both sides of her mouth. God knows what she thought of me. I really wanted to stay downstairs. It felt warmer even though the heating wasn't on. Then Mum just started crying, and said, 'Aw, love,' and she came across the kitchen like she was going to hug me, but I couldn't let her touch what I am, touch *this*. I knew how hard it was for her having me instead of a daughter, so I just said, 'I'm sorry, I'm sorry,' and then I ran upstairs and she followed me and she sat outside my door crying and I sat inside crying. We stayed like that, crying together, for ages, the door between us. Mum went downstairs but came running back up, and said, 'Yer tea's here, love.' When I looked, it was more than tea. It was sandwiches and cigarettes and crisps and a big bar of chocolate and a can of coke.

I'm having another fag. Mum said she'll get me some more today so hopefully she won't forget. I had a dream about Dad last night. Mental it was. He was an opera singer, he was singing as he beat me. Singing Italian, for Christ's sake. He can't even speak fucking Gaelic for all he talks about being fucking Irish.

What did you say? Am I scared about tomorrow? Piss off. I'm not fucking scared but do you have to keep going on about it all the time? Fuck you and fuck your questions. Stick them up your arse. I'm so fucking sick of all this talking. I don't need you or anyone. I hate you all. Fuck off and don't bother coming back.

Part Nine
Right Now

I'm sorry for shouting at you before. I don't want to talk anymore, let's just sit for a bit. You can watch the sun coming up with me. I've always liked dawn. It's the end of the night, with all its scary dark corners, but it's before everyone's awake. I could pretend to be anything in that tiny tube of time. I used to pretend I was on my way to see the world. I wish I had Bonnie with me. I could talk to her or just lie on the bed and she'd be all warm and soft against me. I was going to get her last night but I didn't have the bottle to open the door. I only had to get down the goddamn stairs but I couldn't do it. And now I won't see her again. I hope Mum looks after her properly, after I've gone.

I remember once when my brothers were out and it was just me and Dad, and I was helping him to do the crossword. He always struggled with it, every day, writing in the wrong words and then writing over them until there was no more space to write in anymore. One time he asked me and when I told him, he wrote it in. And then he asked me another and another and then we'd finished it. He folded the paper up so that it was kind of square, framing the crossword and put it on the coffee table and he kept looking at it and smiling. I've still got that crossword somewhere. I cut it out before Mum threw the paper away.

I know people are trying to help me but I don't know why anyone bothers. I saw my file on Mr Broeder's desk once. He went out to speak to a secretary and I had a look at it. I only saw one page because I was scared he'd come back. It had a picture of me and Tommo and Jamie, from years and years before – the one Dad took of us in the back garden where he got really angry because we weren't smiling enough. On the paper it said *At risk of serious injury or death*. At risk of never growing up. At risk from our own dad, who could hate us for long enough to kill us.

I know what I am. I am a name typed on a form in a file inside a drawer at the back of an office. I am a document tutted over by people who go home and love their kids. I'm a fifteen-year-old smear on the arse of society. I am something not right, something broken down and busted, something to be put away and forgotten. All the ideas I had in my head – you've not even heard the best of them – and now they're going to take me to the council dump for kids. I know what they do. They lock you up and shove a needle full of dope into you to handcuff your brain and then you're slobbering in a corner. No more trouble from you. But I've got a secret weapon, of course. This little bit of mirror that is coming right along with me. I've got some plans of my own now so I guess we should say bye. I'm going to disappear. Easy as that. Game over. The end. Like I said before, things like me, deformed, forgotten things, we don't have a future. We just have a day when we no longer wake up.

Acknowledgements

To my sisters and brothers Carol, Christine, Mick and Ste who once made sorrow bearable. To my nieces Erin, Ellie and Connie and nephew, Rory, source of much joy. To mum for being 'Ama-la'. To Sheila and Teresa who taught me kindness. To Jag for his love and forgiveness. To George, for his ability to breach my defences and teach me. To Clio, without whose help and encouragement this book would never have been finished. To my brother Mick, for reading the complete first draft. To my friends - I don't see enough of you.

My heartfelt thanks to the wonderful team at Legend Press for their excellent work and brilliant support and to the Luke Bitmead Foundation and judging panel for believing in my novel. And to Elaine, a remarkable, lovely woman who has made all this possible.

And finally, to Tashi. Our soul-deep friendship keeps me going. I couldn't do it without you. For everything – tu-chen-na.

Lyn G. Farrell grew up in Lancashire where she would have gone to school if life had been different. She spent most of her teenage years reading anything she could get her hands on.

She studied Psychology at the University of Leeds and now works in the School of Education at Leeds Beckett University.

Lyn is the winner of the 2015 Luke Bitmead Burary and *The Wacky Man* is her debut novel.

You can contact Lyn via Twitter
@FarrellWrites

The Wacky Man was the
Winner of the 2015 Luke Bitmead Bursary

The award was set up shortly after Luke's death in 2006 by his family to support and encourage the work of fledgling novel writers. The top prize is a publishing contract with Legend Press, as well as a cash bursary.

We are delighted to be working with Luke's family to ensure that Luke's name and memory lives on – not only through his work, but through this wonderful memorial bursary too. For those of you lucky enough to have met Luke you will know that he was hugely compassionate and would love the idea of another struggling talented writer being supported on the arduous road to securing their first publishing deal.

We will ensure that, as with all our authors, we give the winner of the bursary as much support as we can, and offer them the most effective creative platform from which to showcase their talent. We can't wait to start reading and judging the submissions.

We are pleased to be continuing this brilliant bursary for a ninth year, and hope to follow in the success of our previous winners Andrew Blackman (*On the Holloway Road*, February 2009), Ruth Dugdall (*The Woman Before Me*, August 2010), Sophie Duffy (*The Generation Game*, August 2011), J.R. Crook (*Sleeping Patterns*, July 2012), Joanne Graham (*Lacey's House*, May 2013), Jo Gatford (*White Lies*, July 2014) Tara Guha (*Untouchable Things*, September 2015) and Lyn G. Farrell (*The Wacky Man*, May 2016).

For more information on the bursary and all
Legend Press titles visit:
www.legendpress.co.uk
Follow us @legend_press